THE WORLD OF
MIGHT&MAGIC

UBISOFT

First published in Great Britain in 2012 by Osprey Publishing,
Midland House, West Way, Botley, Oxford, OX2 0PH, UK
44–02 23rd St, Suite 219, Long Island City, NY 11101, USA

E-mail: info@ospreypublishing.com

Osprey Publishing is part of the Osprey Group

A CIP catalogue record for this book is available from the British Library

Print ISBN: 978 1 78096 864 3

Page layout and cover design by Myriam Bell Design, UK
Typeset in ITC Benguiat and Ashan
Originated by PDQ Digital Media Solutions Ltd., Suffolk, UK
Printed in China through Worldprint Ltd.

12 13 14 15 16   10 9 8 7 6 5 4 3 2 1

www.ospreypublishing.com

Osprey Publishing is supporting the Woodland Trust, the UK's leading woodland
conservation charity, by funding the dedication of trees.

CONTENTS

INTRODUCTION

The Might & Magic saga started in 1986 by New World Computing with the release of *Might & Magic Book 1: Secret of the Inner Sanctum*. It was a first-person, computer role-playing game set in a medieval fantasy universe, in the tradition of classics like Wizardry or The Bard's Tale – but instead of confining the player to some obscure maze of caves and dungeons, Might & Magic featured a vast open world, with forests, mountains, castles and cities, a land of mysteries and wonders

In 1996 New World Computing became a subsidiary of The 3DO Company. In 2003, after the closure of 3DO, the rights to Might and Magic were purchased by Ubisoft. Ubisoft was no stranger to Might & Magic. For years the French company had been publishing the Might & Magic games in Europe.

One of the hard decisions Ubisoft had to take was putting aside the old universe for a new setting: the world of Ashan. Like its predecessors Terra and Enroth, Ashan offers its own background and flavour while staying true to the pillars of what made Might & Magic unique and compelling: its factions, rich bestiary, epic storylines and enchanted atmosphere.

Ashan is a world where the forces of Order and Chaos wage an endless battle through their respective Dragon-Gods and mortal servants.

It is also a crucible in which the talent and passion of the artists, designers, writers, coders and producers from the Ubisoft teams are mixed to concoct inspiring and appealing stories, landscapes, creatures and heroes.

The book you are holding in your hands is the sum of their numerous artistic and creative endeavours. You are only a step away from partaking in their glorious adventures. All you need to do is turn the page...

BOOK OF ECLIPSES
HISTORY OF ASHAN

The World of ASHAN

CIRCA 564 YSD

SEA OF SHADOWS

IRISUS SEA

SAVAGE SEA

JADE OCEAN

GRIMHEIM

RANAAR

NARSHIMA

PAO ISLANDS

NERESH

HOLY EMPIRE

IROLLAN

YGG CHALL

SILVER CITIES

RANAAR

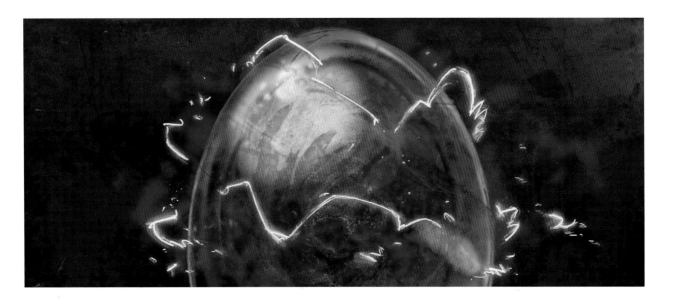

THE MYTHIC AGE

THE COSMIC EGG AND THE PRIMORDIAL TWINS

In the beginning there was Magic and the Void. Magic formed itself into the Cosmic Egg. Inside the Egg the Dragon twins Asha and Urgash, Sister and Brother, Order and Chaos, were nurtured with Primordial Magic until they hatched. Spawned from Magic to exist amidst the Void, the Primordial Dragons were the first with the potential to harness its unlimited power.

While the brother, Urgash, basked in Magic's infinite possibilities, dreaming of its potential for unlimited freedom, the sister, Asha, decided to give it shape and purpose.

THE COLOURS OF MAGIC

Asha defined and named six "colours" of Magic that she had identified floating amongst the cosmic Void. They were Darkness, Light, Earth, Fire, Water, and Air. These were the threads with which she would weave the universe.

THE ELEMENTAL DRAGONS

Asha gave birth to six Dragon Children, manifestations of the colours of Magic, to both guide and rule her creation. Malassa daughter of Darkness, Elrath son of Light, Sylanna daughter of Earth, Arkath son of Fire, Shalassa daughter of Water and Ylath son of Air.

ASHAN

Together with her children, Asha created Ashan, a world formed amidst the Darkness, bathed by the Light of the sun, an orb of Earth warmed by a heart of Fire, cooled by veins and arteries of Water, breathed to life by currents of Air. Their work complete, the Dragons paused to gaze at their creation, and Asha was pleased.

THE ELDER RACES

Asha now decided to create servants for her Dragon children. These Elder races were also emanations of the colours of Magic: the Faceless of Darkness, the Angels of Light, the Elves of Earth, the Dwarves of Fire, the Nagas of Water, and the Humans of Air.

To give them sentience and grant them the ability to use Magic, Asha baptized them in the blood of their respective patron Dragon, so that it would mix with their own and flow in their veins.

THE CHILDREN OF CHAOS

Urgash looked upon the Elemental Dragons and the world that Asha had made, and he was filled with envy and disgust. What his sister had created, he would destroy. What she had organized, he would unravel and corrupt.

In mockery of the Elder races, Urgash spawned the Demons, a race of alien creatures who live in a constant state of change, yielding to every urge they felt no matter how base. To impose some semblance of authority over his unruly, vicious offspring, Urgash created six Demon Overlords, twisted counterparts to the Elemental Dragons. Each Overlord was given dominion over a different aspect of Urgash's unbridled passions.

THE WARS OF CREATION

Order and Chaos collided during what would later be called the "Wars of Creation". This was an all-out conflict, fought on all levels of reality. Led by Urgash and the Overlords, the Demons confronted the Elder races and their patron Dragons. The forces of Order were ultimately victorious.

Urgash, vanquished but not destroyed, was banished and jailed in Ashan's fiery core, and his monstrous offsprings fled to the far corners of the world. Lurking in uninhabited places, they slowly gather their strength. When Asha

THE DRAGONBLOOD CRYSTALS AND NEXUSES

As the Dragon-Gods fought against each other, their blood fell over Ashan. It formed a network of dragon veins that, with the passing of time, crystallized into magical nodes. These Dragon Nexuses, as they became know, changed the nature of Ashan forever.

Their Magical aura turned normal plants and animals into supernatural creatures, imbued with a fraction of the power of the Dragon Gods.

laid her eyes on the devastation brought to her creation and on the wounds received by her children, she shed myriad tears that cleansed the world of the corruption of Chaos. But this rejuvenation came at a terrible price.

THE SPIRIT WORLD AND THE VEIL

The tears of Asha split her creation in two. First, the material world which would be subject to the cycle of Time, of Life and Death, of the seasons and the passage of night and day. And second, the spirit world, which would be a mirror-image of Ashan before it was corrupted by Chaos, perfect and unchanging. The two worlds would be separated by the "Veil", a magical gate, an antechamber filled with dreams, ghosts and frozen memories.

The Dragons would inhabit the spirit world, leaving their servant races forlorn on the other side of the Veil. Death was created as a blessing, to terminate the agony of the countless victims of the War of Creation and allow them to find peace.

Severely weakened by this cosmic-scale ritual, Asha wove a cocoon around herself and fell into a restorative torpor. The cocoon's reflection in the material world was called the Moon, and its various aspects became yet another marker for the cycle of Time.

The creation of the Veil marks the end of the Mythic Age and the dawn of the Ancient Age.

THE ANCIENT AGE

THE SHANTIRI EMPIRE

From the Spirit world, the Dragon Gods send visions to their now mortal servants, instructing them in proper worship. This leads to the foundation of the Shantiri Empire which unifies all six Elder races into a single nation, ruled by a cast of Priests, led by nine Hierophants (one per Elemental Dragon, three for Asha to represent her various aspects).

Through their prayers and sacrifice, the Shantiri devouts hope to restore the power of their Gods so they could someday return. The Shantiris spread across the face of the world, building titanic cities and temples.

THE ELDER WARS

The Angels, children of the Light, fight the Faceless, children of Darkness, in a genocidal war. The Angels seek retribution on the Faceless for their betrayal in the Wars of Creation. The destruction is terrible, both races brought to the brink of extinction. The Shantiri civilization suffers from the collateral damage. In a single night, most inhabitants of the Shantiri Empire vanish, and their cities are cast down. Only ruins remain. The survivors flee all over Ashan. The Faceless are blamed.

In the coming centuries, Shantiri will be slowly forgotten, and most of its magical knowledge lost. The Shantiri ruins gain a reputation for being haunted.

SAR-ELAM, THE SEVENTH DRAGON

The mysterious Human prophet Sar-Elam undertakes a mystical quest, travels through the Spirit World, and reaches the conscience of Asha, who teaches him about the nature of matter and spirit and shows him the higher path of power. Enlightened by his new understanding, Sar-Elam becomes the Seventh Dragon...

THE HISTORICAL AGE

YEARS OF THE SEVENTH DRAGON (YSD)

0 YSD – THE REVELATION OF THE SEVENTH DRAGON

Sar-Elam's ascension to Dragonhood marks the dawn of the Historical Age. From now on time on Ashan will be counted and referred to in the historians' chronicles as "Years of the Seventh Dragon" (YSD).

0 YSD - THE TWILIGHT COVENANT

Upon his return to Ashan, Sar Elam's first act as a Dragon God is to gather the leaders of the Angels and the Faceless. Using his newfound powers and authority, he imposes a peace treaty that will be known as the Twilight Covenant.

To avoid a mutual genocide, and another "Shantiri disaster", Angels and Faceless are forced to swear a magical oath that will prevent them from using their magic to harm each other. This pact is enforced by powerful primordial magic that cannot be broken by anything short of a Dragon God.

The majority of the surviving Angels and Faceless gladly accept the oath, as they see it as their last chance for survival. It helps that the more fanatic and warlike among them have perished. It is time to mourn their fallen brothers and sisters and to rebuild their shattered kingdoms, not to continue the bloodshed.

0 YSD - THE YOUNG KINGDOMS

After the fall of the Shantiri Empire, the Elder races grow apart. Establishment of Angel cities in the clouds, Faceless retreats in the darkest places of Ashan, Dwarf fortresses deep in the Grimheim mountains, Elf tree-towns in the forests of Irollan, Naga palaces at the bottom of the Jade Ocean, and Human settlements in the central plains of Ashan.

The Demons take advantage of the ensuing confusion to leave their hideouts and re-establish a foothold in Ashan, lurking in uninhabited places and slowly gathering their strength.

THE HOLY FALCON EMPIRE

CIRCA 564 YSD

RANAAR

HERESH

IROLLAN

STORMCLIFF

WOLF DUCHY

STONEHELM

NILSHAVEN

FLAMMSCHREIN

GRIFFIN DUCHY

EASTALON

BULL DUCHY

LISTMOOR

STAG DUCHY

IMPERIAL PROVINCE

CHIAROSCURO

HORNCREST

FALCON'S REACH

GREYHOUND DUCHY

ERIDAN'S CROSSING

UNICORN DUCHY

YORWICK

WHITECLIFF

3 YSD — THE FALCON EMPIRE

Ronan the Great, High King of the Falcon clan, unifies the squabbling Human tribes of the plains through a combination of dazzling generalship, brilliant negotiation, and the occasional political marriage.

Ronan declares the foundation of the Falcon Empire and settles in to make his position as Emperor hereditary.

The Seventh Dragon blesses the new monarch and prophesies that the Falcon line shall endure as long as the world does.

28-40 YSD — THE WARS OF FIRE

This is the first and greatest Demon incursion in historical times. Rising from their hidden dens, the children of Chaos rage across the land to wreak vengeance on the servants of the Dragons. The worst of their ire is focused on the Angels, weakened by the Elder Wars and the Twilight Covenant.

Sar-Elam unites all of the Elder races against the Demon threat.

40 YSD — THE SACRIFICE OF THE SEVENTH DRAGON

Through the resignation of all his recurring lifetimes and for the protection of all of Ashan, Sar-Elam sacrifices himself to repel the Demon invasion. He exhausts his nearly god-like powers in one incandescent spell to cast the Demons out of this world and prevent their return. His own soul is consumed and woven into a mystical barrier that seals the Demons into the fiery core of Ashan, near their Progenitor Urgash, the Dragon of Chaos.

Thus were the Demons bound up in a prison-world of eternal fire that would later be called Sheogh, for what the people of Ashan thought would be eternity...

48 YSD — THE FALCON EMPIRE BECOMES THE HOLY EMPIRE

During the Wars of Fire, the Demons bring down the sky-cities of the Angels, and most of the Children of the Light perish.

The Angels are in a dire predicament. Their numbers had been declining for centuries because of their courageous but often deadly exploits during the Wars of Creation and the Elder Wars and their low rate of reproduction. They are facing the end of their race and, consequently, an end to the worship of their patron Dragon-God, Elrath. So they search for nations to convert and they set their eyes on the Humans of the young Falcon Empire, lost in the religious upheaval that had followed Sar-Elam's ascension to Dragonhood and the Wars of Fire.

The Angels approach the young boy Brian, great-grandson to Ronan Falcon, and help him convert his fragile Empire, forlorn by the fickle Dragon of Air, into a strong nation dedicated to the stern and unforgiving Dragon of Light.

In 48 YSD, as Brian is crowned Emperor, he gives absolute power to the Church of Elrath. The Human kingdom is renamed "Holy Falcon Empire".

48 YSD — THE OATH OF THE SEVEN SWORDS OF VIRTUE

As a gift to their new "vassals", the Angels offer seven magical swords, symbolizing the seven virtues of Elrath. The Holy Empire contains six Duchies, so one sword is given to each Duke. The seventh, and most powerful, is reserved for the Emperor.

DEMON CULTS

From this moment on, the repercussions of the Demon invasion will echo through the world in the form of sects, cults, and spies.

THE SKULL OF SHADOWS

Sar-Elam began life as a Human prophet. In fact, he was the first and the most powerful Wizard that ever lived. As he transcended the gap between mortal-human and immortal-dragon in becoming the Seventh Dragon, he also gained the ability to change into a draconic form.

When he died in the process of creating the prison world of Sheogh, a fragment of his soul was split and bound to a huge chunk of shadowsteel ore, that was later shaped like a dragon skull to honour his "divine" (draconic) essence.

This relic, later called the "Skull of Shadows", was hidden away by servants of Asha for centuries, ready for the day it would be needed again. All records of its location were destroyed.

48 YSD — THE FIRST FREE CITIES

Dissent grows among many imperial citizens who resent being forced to abandon Ylath. Some will leave the Empire's territory to found the first Free Cities. Over the centuries, other Free Cities will arise, most of them open to all races and religions of Ashan.

50-260 YSD — THE YEARS OF HEALING

Reconstruction from the Wars of Fire and relatively harmonious relations between the races.

62 YSD — THE SCHISM OF THE SEVEN

Founding of the Church of Asha, the Dragon Knights, and the Seven Cities

Schism between the disciples of Sar-Elam, who can't agree on the best way to follow the road laid down by the Seventh Dragon and hopefully someday surpass him.

Three Disciples, led by Sar-Antor, found the Church of Asha, dedicated to the worship of the Dragon of Order. The cult has a religious approach to Sar-Elam's teachings. It is composed of three different congregations, one for each face of Asha: the White Weavers (nurses and midwives), the Blind Brothers (seers and chroniclers), and the Silent Sisters (undertakers and embalmers).

Sar-Badon founds the Dragon Knights, a more mystical and martial order, disciplined in both body and mind. The other disciples, led by Sar-Shazzar, the most gifted of them all, lead an exodus of like-minded followers into the southern deserts of Sahaar. Their approach is more scholarly. Magic for them does not equate to Faith. It is simply a higher form of knowledge that must be developed through extensive study of arcane lore (mainly the teachings of Sar-Elam). They will eventually found the Seven Cities, the first Wizard kingdom.

67 YSD — THE PROPHECY OF THE DARK MESSIAH

Sar-Shazzar gives the Prophecy of the Dark Messiah, which predicts, among other things, that a chosen half-Human, half-Demon, born to a Demon Lord and a faultless Human maiden, will someday shatter the walls of Sheogh and unleash the vengeful legions of Chaos on the world.

74 YSD — MYSTERIOUS DEATH OF SAR-SHAZZAR

Sar-Shazzar dies in his sleep. When attendants attempt to move his body to the crypt for preparation and burial, it crumbles to ashes.

104 YSD — THE DRAGON KNIGHTS BECOME A SECRET ORDER

On his deathbed, Sar-Badon commands the Dragon Knights to build the Hidden Houses and to retreat to them when they are complete. These fortified monasteries are scattered across the world, dedicated to preserving the teachings of the Seventh Dragon, watching against any Demon activity, and training new Dragon Knights to fill their ranks.

No longer are the Dragon Knights to be prominent or visible in the world. Through the centuries, they will leave their strongholds only rarely and only in times of extreme danger.

330 YSD — FIRST ECLIPSE
WAR OF THE BLOOD MOON

A total lunar eclipse provokes a massive rupture of the Demon Prison. The Demon legions force their way out and ravage across Irollan. Caught by surprise, the Elves are rapidly overwhelmed. Great swaths of their sacred forests are burned away by the Demons, scarring the land and poisoning the waters.

Human and Dwarf armies are rallied, but they too fail to contain the raving legions of Chaos.

335 YSD — CREATION OF THE ORCS

In a desperate attempt to prevent the Demon hordes from overrunning the known world, the Wizards of the Seven Cities achieved perhaps their greatest hubris, the creation of the Orcs. In the laboratories of Al-Rubit, the Crimson Wizards experiment with Demon blood, which they inoculate into Human slaves and criminals.

The Goblins are created first, using the blood of minor Demons, and the result is considered a failure. The Cyclopes are created next, using the blood of major Demons and, though the result is spectacular, the giants prove too unruly to be dependable.

The right mixture is finally found and the Orcs are created. They also prove capable of leading the Goblins and Cyclopes in battle.

336 YSD — DEFEAT OF THE DEMON LEGIONS

The Orc shock troops become the decisive weapon in the War of the Blood Moon, turning the tide of the conflict and saving Ashan from total destruction. The Demons are finally cast down and banished back to their prison.

336 YSD — DISCOVERY OF THE ECLIPSE CYCLE

Shocked by the power of the Demon outbreak, the wisest sages of Ashan investigate and discover that Sar-Elam's spiritual prison has a built-in flaw. During a lunar eclipse, when the Moon (Asha's

THE NAGAS' ISOLATIONISM

During the War of the Blood Moon, the Nagas remained apart, meditating in isolation. The turmoil of the conflict was therefore only heard as echoes and rumours.

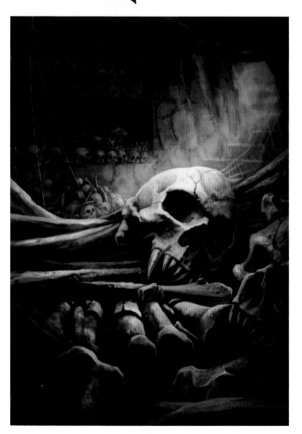

cocoon) is shadowed by Ashan (Urgash's prison), the walls of Sheogh are weakened sufficiently for the Demons to escape.

As a result, the Blind Brothers decide to keep a constant watch. They create massive predictive timetables, and they discover that another lunar eclipse isn't due for another 200 years.

336 YSD — THE CLEANSING OF IROLLAN

Once the fighting is over, the Elves retreat to their wounded kingdom and spend almost two centuries restoring it, planting new groves, cleansing the waters, and expelling the slightest bit of Demon taint from their lands.

336 YSD — ENSLAVEMENT OF THE ORCS

In the wake of the War of the Blood Moon, a terrible decision is made on the fate of the surviving Orcs. Now that the danger has passed, they are resettled as slaves and indentured troops to work the mines and guard dangerous borders in the Seven Cities and the neighbouring Holy Falcon Empire.

Persecuted and feared, never truly accepted, they grow bitter and resentful towards those whom they see as the favoured children of the Dragon Gods.

340-350 YSD — CREATION OF THE BEASTMEN

Bolstered by the success of their creations, the Crimson Wizards grow to a position of dominance within the political classes of the Seven Cities. But Orcs are not the only results of their experiments. Around the same time, they combine Humans with various animals by exposing them to powerful Dragon Nexuses.

The results are various species that will be referred to as "Beastmen" (Centaurs, Minotaurs, Harpies, Mermaids, Rakshasas, etc.). Their stated purpose is to replace the Orcs as workers, servants, guards and playthings in the Seven Cities. The Beastmen are considered superior evolutions over the Orcs because they contain no Demon blood.

461 YSD — DISCOVERY OF NECROMANCY

Belketh, a disciple of Sar-Shazzar, discovers a fragmented copy of the Revelation of the Seventh Dragon, which details the worship of Asha through its least understood and most feared aspect. Belketh is struck by the conviction that he has found the higher path to the power of the immortal soul. He will call it "Necromancy".

Necromantic experimentations begin in Belketh's city, Al-Betyl. Soon, the first Undead servants (ghosts and animated corpses) rise from the grave to replace the Beastmen and Orcs. Even though the morbid nature of Necromancy is very controversial, it is welcomed by many as a way to become less dependent on the now formidable economic and military power of the Crimson Wizards. The Undead servants come from a never-ending source, are ever-obedient, know no fear, have no need to rest or feed, and possess no desire to rebel.

467-470 YSD — THE ORC REBELLION

After more than a century of oppression, the long-restive Orc population rises up against its creators. Born in Shahibdiya, the rebellion, led by the legendary Kunyak, quickly spreads to the whole of the Seven Cities and to the Holy Falcon Empire. More than half of the Beastmen rebel with the Orcs. The repression is brutal, and though the Orcs and their allied Beastmen fight fiercely, they are relentlessly driven back.

Eventually, the broken, but unrepentant survivors flee to the most inhospitable reaches of the world, mainly the deserts of Sahaar (South), the steppes of Ranaar (North-East), and the Pao Islands (Jade Ocean, South-East). Once settled in their new territories, the separate Orc nations will develop unique cultures and languages, but they will all share common values of pride, courage and independence. And their hatred for the Demons, their Wizard creators and the Holy Empire will never die.

470-504 YSD — THE ORC CRUSADES

When the Orcs rebelled, they declared themselves free of their masters and of the Dragon Gods, unwilling to kneel in obedience or worship. This blasphemy could not be borne by the Holy Empire, and its retaliation was swift. In 470 YSD, Emperor Connor I declares a holy crusade against the Orcs.

For about thirty years, Imperial armies chase the Orcs down to their isolated refuges and attempt to subjugate them and convert them back to Dragon worship.

479 YSD — THE CREATION OF THE CONSTRUCTS

The Wizards of Al-Safir, inspired by ancient Shantiri art, create the constructs: Golems, Gargoyles and Titans of various sorts. These are considered an ideal solution to replace the Orc and Beastmen slaves, and the unsettling Undead puppets of the Necromancers.

490 YSD — THE SEVEN CITIES SPLIT INTO 4 HOUSES

The recent political dissensions within the Seven Cities divide the Wizards into four Orders.

House Anima, based in Al-Imral, gathers the Summoners, loyal to the old ways of Magic, the summoning and binding of Spirits.

House Chimera, based in Al-Rubit and governed by the Crimson Wizards, creators of the Orcs and the Beastmen, leads the Shapers, who experiment with mutant lifeforms by exposing various creatures (including representatives of the Elders races, usually slaves or convicts) to the powerful radiations of the Dragon Nexuses.

House Eterna, based in Al-Betyl and led by Belketh, commands the Necromancers, masters of the Undead.

House Materia, based in Al-Safir, unites the Alchemists, builders of the Constructs.

504 YSD — THE END OF THE ORC CRUSADES

The Falcon Empress Morwenna commands her armada to set sail for the Pao islands on the Jade Ocean, with the declared intent to capture or exterminate the local Orc population to the last child. But a magical storm of tremendous magnitude sinks the imperial fleet, and the Empress with it.

The new Emperor, Connor III, Morwenna's son, declares this a sign from the Dragons and formally ends the Orc Crusades.

510 YSD — THE BLIND BROTHERS PREDICT THE SECOND BLOOD-MOON ECLIPSE

The date for the Second Eclipse, and the ensuing Demon invasion, is set for 565 YSD. The Blind Brothers contact the leaders of all the nations of Ashan and ask them to prepare for war.

521 YSD — MIRACULOUS RETURN OF THE ARCHANGEL MICHAEL

Michael, the legendary Angel general slain by a Faceless assassin during the Elder Wars, reappears in Ashan. The exact nature of his resurrection is unknown but attributed by most to Elrath himself, as a gift to the Holy Empire to help them defeat the Demons in the upcoming Eclipse.

Michael is appalled by the changes he discovers in the world since his death. Angels and Faceless have been diminished in number and power through the Twilight Covenant. Demons have been locked in Sheogh by a certain Sar-Elam who considers himself to be equal to the Dragon Gods. Orcs, half-Demon and half-Human, roam freely throughout the realms of the Holy Empire with apparent impunity... Michael also learns of the impeding Eclipse, but he is less worried by the Demons than by his former enemies, the Faceless.

537 YSD — ARNIEL'S REFORM

His head turned by a band of flatterers, High King Arniel decides that Elf power is too decentralized, and that the traditional way of electing the supreme ruler (through a vision shared by the Druids) is unreliable. His solution is to usurp the powers of the local Elf kings, strip the Druids of their authority and make his own title hereditary.

537 YSD — TUIDHANA'S SECESSION

Outraged by Arniel's proclamations, Queen Tuidhana, leader of a small Elf nation that lives at the north-western border of the Holy Empire, declares herself independent from the High King.

538 YSD — MICHAEL BECOMES CHIEF WAR COUNCILLOR OF THE HOLY EMPIRE

Michael becomes chief war councillor for the Emperor Liam Falcon, and convinces him to view with distrust and suspicion not only the Faceless, but also the Orcs ("Demons"), the Wizards and the Necromancers ("Heretics"), and even the Elves (he gathers clues indicating that Queen Tuidhana's Elves are dealing with the Faceless).

540 YSD — WAR OF THE BITTER ASHES

Emperor Liam Falcon sees Tuidhana's kingdom as vulnerable and attempts to annex it. Battered by the imperial armies, Tuidhana appeals to Irollan for help but is refused. Only when it looks like the Humans will gain a foothold in Elven territory does the High King launch a counter-attack – one with the intent of bringing Tuidhana's land back into the fold.

541 YSD — CREATION OF THE DARK ELVES

Desperate to protect her people, Tuidhana turns to the few surviving Faceless. They are willing to help her for a price. If she would turn herself and her people to the worship of Malassa, Dragon of Darkness, then the Faceless would grant her the power she needs. Tuidhana accepts their offer. The Dark Elves are born.

548 YSD — THE PEACE OF NEW SPRING

With the newfound powers granted by her Faceless allies, Tuidhana reaffirms her independence. Her kingdom's freedom is recognized – at swordpoint – by Elves and Humans.

An uneasy peace settles between the Elves and the Dark Elves. Elf emissaries are turned away at the border. The Holy Falcon Empire forfeits any claim to Tuidhana's lands and makes extensive reparations. Intermittent hostilities persist across the borders, but twenty years will pass in a rough truce, until a terrible accident sends things from bad to worse…

564 YSD – SECOND ECLIPSE
RISE OF THE DEMON SOVEREIGN

The Demons unexpectedly return several years before the date predicted by the Blind Brothers. This time, the children of Chaos focus their rampage on the Holy Empire. Its capital, Falcon's Reach, is nearly razed to the ground. Emperor Liam is killed and succeeded by his niece, Gwendolyn.

The Demons are ultimately defeated by an improbable coalition of imperial knights, Naga armies, Undead legions sent by Necromancers of the Seven Cities, and free Orcs from the Pao islands. Oddly enough, in the aftermath of the conflict, the names of the six Demon Overlords, Urgash's Champions, are heard no more.

A single Sovereign rises to take their place. His origins obscure, his face a mystery, he will only be referred to as Kha-Beleth…

566 YSD — DAY OF THE TEARS OF FIRE — DESTRUCTION OF BRYTHIGGA AND DEATH OF ARNIEL

Brythigga, the Mother of Trees, is set on fire in the centre of the Elf capital. The sacred tree is burned to the ground, leaving a blackened scar on the earth where nothing will ever grow again.

Arniel and his family are caught inside the conflagration. None survive. The Dark Elves are blamed for the heinous crime.

566 YSD — DEATH OF TUIDHANA

In a gesture of mercy, Vaniel, Arniel's successor, offers Tuidhana safe passage out of Irollan. For one week, he will hold back the forces howling for vengeance. Her people can leave in safety, providing they accept exile and never return. After that time, he will personally lead his armies across her kingdom and wipe out all the remaining Dark Elves.

As the Elf armies stay their attack, Tuidhana urges her people to find safety elsewhere. Led by Tuidhana's children and some Faceless guides, most of them go east, eventually settling underground, on the Dwarf border. Tuidhana remains behind with only a handful of loyal followers to stand against the Elf armies massed on her border. She dies a queen and a martyr, defending her lands.

585 YSD — DISCOVERY OF DEMON IMPLICATION IN BRYTHIGGA'S DESTRUCTION

Vaniel eventually discovers that Demons were involved in the burning of Brythigga. He decides to apologize to Tuidhana's people. Emissaries are sent from Irollan to the wandering Dark Elves, offering amnesty and inviting them to return home, but they unanimously refuse...

586-702 YSD — WAR UNDER THE MOUNTAINS

As the first Dark Elves settle on the Dwarves' borders, the relations between the two races start tense and get worse. Both seek many of the same

---

THE NEW MOTHER OF TREES

The place where Brythigga had stood was stricken from the maps, and to this day no Elf will go there. Another Mother of Trees has been consecrated, hidden deep within the forests, but no Elf will speak of her to outsiders.

resources in the dark deeps, and intersections between tunnels bring short, sharp fights. Very soon, the skirmishes grow into an open conflict.

The so-called War Under the Mountains is brutal, completely devoid of mercy, as massive armies clash in the dark. Eventually, the Dwarves, led by Hathor Deepstrider Orlandsson, crush the Dark Elves and drive them out.

THE DARK ELF SOULSCAR CLAN TURNS TO DEMON WORSHIP

As the War Under the Mountain turns against the Dark Elves, exiled Demonists from the Seven Cities make contact with Tuidhana's people. Like the Faceless before them, they offer assistance in exchange for worship of their Dragon-God, Urgash.

The Dark Elves leaders reject the offer, except Raelag, Tuidhana's elder son, who signs a pact with the Demon cultists. His clan, the Soulscar, turns to secret Demon worship.

702 YSD — YGG-CHALL, THE DARK ELF KINGDOM

Repelled by the Dwarves, the Dark Elves move south, deep within the mountains. Guided by their Faceless allies, they finally settle on the ruins of the ancient Faceless kingdom of Ygg-Chall. They organize themselves into several clans, each led by a child of Tuidhana.

717 YSD — THIRD ECLIPSE
DRAGON HUNT

The Third eclipse is brief. This time the Blind Brothers had correctly predicted it, and the various nations of Ashan are well prepared and quick to react. Only a small band of Demons manages to escape into the world. They seek out the hidden strongholds of the Dragon Knights and begin a bloody secret war. The Dragon Knights are eventually victorious.

751-770 YSD — PURGE OF THE NECROMANCERS CIVIL WAR IN THE SEVEN CITIES

Jealous of the power acquired by the Necromancers, the Wizards of the Seven Cities initiate a large-scale persecution, ranging from the seizing of their properties, to banishment, to the spectacle of public executions.

A long and gruesome civil war ensues. The Necromancers are finally defeated and forced to settle in the valleys of Heresh. They declare their independence, using the city of Nar-Heresh as their base of operations to plan their revenge.

756 YSD — DEATH OF VANIEL, HIGH KING OF THE ELVES

Vaniel dies in 756 and is succeeded by Alaron. The new High King's eye turns away from the forest, and he slowly re-establishes stronger ties with the other nations. He provides aid to the Wizards of the Silver Cities in their wars against the Necromancers and encourages traders to come to the Elf borders.

771 YSD — FOUNDATION OF THE SILVER LEAGUE

The Wizards have won the war against the Necromancers but at a steep cost. They have to modify the borders of their kingdom. Lamenting their lost "golden age", they name their new home the Silver Cities. Their central seat of power becomes Al-Safir, home of the Alchemists, now the dominant Wizard House.

776 YSD — THE CRIMSON WIZARDS OF KARTHAL

Some of the Wizards, disgruntled with the jurisdiction of their peers, choose voluntary exile and leave for the trackless wilds. Most sell themselves as rogue mages to the Free Cities. But the Crimson Wizards of Al-Rubit and their Beastmen servants, now rejected in favour of the Constructs, settle to the west, and found the city of Karthal on the coast of the Irisus Sea. Their armies carve out a small territory between the mountains of the Dark Elves and the southwest border of the Holy Empire.

813-822 YSD — WAR OF THE BROKEN STAFF

The Necromancers launch a surprise assault on the Silver cities. Undead armies swarm across the borders of Heresh, destroying everything in their path. After ten years of bloody conflict, the Wizards once again gain the upper hand, breaking the Undead legions and scattering their remnants.

The Necromancers are utterly defeated and their kingdom shattered by massive waves of destructive magic. The ancient cities are destroyed and much of the land is rendered uninhabitable. The once fertile valleys of Heresh are "vitrified" and become a barren wasteland, filled with bones and laments. The surviving Necromancers go into hiding. Most retreat underground beneath their destroyed kingdom. Some infiltrate the Holy Empire.

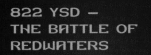

822 YSD — THE BATTLE OF REDWATERS

The War of the Broken Staff ends with the Battle of Redwaters and the death of Belketh.

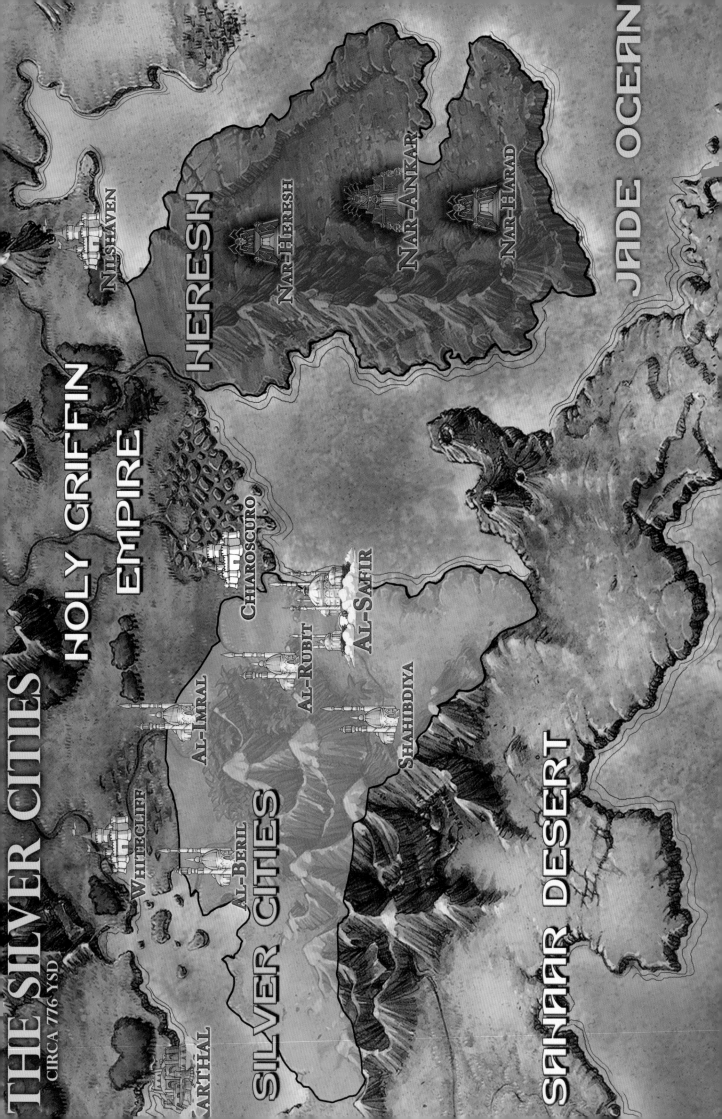

843 YSD — FOURTH ECLIPSE
FALCON'S LAST FLIGHT

Once again, the eclipse's date is accurately foreseen by the Blind Brothers, and very few Demons manage to escape the combined forces of the new Alliance. But a small force of infiltrators and assassins, led by the Succubus Jezebeth, storm the capital of the Falcon Empire and massacre the royal house. Before being murdered, Lady Maeve Falcon manages to send her son Brendan to safety. As soon as the Demons are repelled, a gruesome civil war surges across the Empire, as the various noble houses attempt to claim the throne.

Duke Ivan of the Griffin captures the bloody crown. The Empire is renamed "Holy Griffin Empire".

929 YSD — AZH-RAFIR AND THE BLADE OF BINDING

The Wizard Azh-Rafir, ruler of Al-Imral, converts to Chaos worship. His purpose, however, is not to serve the Demon Sovereign, but to become the "Eighth Dragon", following the path to enlightenment and supreme spiritual power set by Sar-Elam, but by embracing Chaos rather than Order. To accomplish his goal, he needs to recover a legendary sword, called the Blade of Binding, that was forged from one of Urgash's claws, and gives its bearer superior control over the creatures and powers of Chaos.

Azh-Rafir will murder the keepers of the Blade of Binding, including his own wife Delara. His madness is put to an end by his daughter Nadia, his apprentice Cyrus, and the children of the other keepers, Godric, Aidan and Fiona, heirs of the Unicorn Duchy, and the Elf Anwen.

951 YSD — FIFTH ECLIPSE
WAR OF THE GRAY ALLIANCE

The Fifth Eclipse is also predicted by the Blind Brothers. This time, the main battlefield is the desert of Sahaar, at the border of the Silver Cities. The Demon armies are confronted by a combined force of Imperial Knights, Wizards, and Elves. The Dwarves and Nagas are too far from the conflict zone to feel involved, and the Orcs, Dark Elves and Necromancers have unsettled grudges with the forces of the Alliance.

When the war appears lost for the Demons, they retreat to a magic portal that can send them back to Sheogh. Seeing the ultimate victory slipping away, Emperor Alexei IV of the Griffin orders a charge of his knights into the portal, in a final attempt to destroy the Demon Sovereign.

The cautious Alaron, High King of the Elves, hesitates and takes time to ponder, looking for another way. The arrogant Cyrus, Supreme Archmage of the Silver Cities, rejects Alexei's act as utter foolishness and refuses to follow. Alexei does not wait, and he and the cream of Griffin's knighthood perish in Sheogh, under an onslaught of Demons. However, Alexei's soul is rescued by the Dragon Knight Tieru, and bound up in the artefact called the Heart of the Griffin. Alexei leaves his wife Fiona as regent and his first and only son Nicolai, aged 6, as heir.

969 YSD — SIXTH ECLIPSE
QUEEN ISABEL'S WAR

The Griffin Empire is getting ready for a celebration — the marriage of the young Emperor Nicolai to his sweetheart Isabel, Duchess of the Greyhound. The festivities are interrupted, however, by a lunar eclipse not forecast on any calendar. The Demons emerge in force and march towards Talonguard, capital of the Holy Empire.

Like his father twenty years ago, Nicolai bravely faces the Demon legions and dies valiantly at the head of his knights, slain by the Demon Lord Agrael. His young bride will lead the Imperial armies into battle and the ensuing conflict will be known as Queen Isabel's War.

Over the course of the war, Isabel will be manipulated by the Necromancer Markal into murdering the Archmage Cyrus and resurrecting Nicolai as a Vampire. She will also discover that Agrael, Nicolai's killer, is in fact a Dark Elf Demonist who has been watching over her since her birth on order of the Demon Sovereign. Isabel is in fact an important part of Kha-Beleth's masterplan to bring about the Dark Messiah. She has been chosen as the "Dark Madonna", vessel for Kha-Beleth to inseminate her with his child who, being half-Human and half-Demon, would become the Dark Messiah.

Isabel is finally abducted by the Succubus Biara who leads her to Kha Beleth. She is saved by a joint force of heroes, including Godric, the Duke of the Unicorn, Zehir, Cyrus's son and new Supreme Archmage of the Silver Cities, and Agrael, who has fallen in love with Isabel and rebelled against the Demon Sovereign. But they come too late. Her fertilization and pregnancy speeded up by the powers of Chaos, Isabel has already given birth to the Dark Messiah...

970 YSD — THE BIRTH OF THE DARK MESSIAH

Isabel and Kha Beleth's son is delivered to the Demonist Phenrig, who is entrusted with the secret of the boy's heritage. Phenrig's mission is simple — to raise the boy, to train him in the arts of magic and war, to hide him from those who would kill him to prevent the Prophecy of the Dark Messiah, and to set him on the path to fulfil his destiny.

The coming of the Dark Messiah has begun, though none know it yet.

970-973 YSD — THE RED QUEEN ☐ CIVIL WAR IN THE HOLY EMPIRE

Once back in the Holy Empire, Isabel is officially crowned Empress. But she proves to be a cruel and bloody queen. Freyda of the Unicorn, Godric's daughter, joins the rebel coalition led by the young Duke Duncan of the Stag, whose goal is to replace the "usurper" queen by the child Andrei, Nicholai's nephew. Political machinations embroil the Dwarves, the Dark Elves and the Orcs in the conflict.

Andrei is captured and executed by the Empress. It is finally discovered that it is not the real Isabel who sits on the throne, but rather the Succubus Biara, Kha-Beleth's agent. The real Isabel is recovered and she summons allies old and new, including Zehir and his Wizards, to mount an assault on Talonguard and destroy the Demon Queen.

Relinquishing any claim to the throne in order to live out her days in isolation, Isabel crowns Freyda as the new Empress.

972 YSD — ARANTIR'S QUEST FOR THE SKULL OF SHADOWS

It took the Necromancers a couple of centuries to recoup their strength, but in 972 YSD, they rise again as a strong nation under the leadership of the Death Lord Arantir, whose devotion to his goddess, Asha, is matched only by his hatred for her enemies, the Demons.

By investigating the source of the demonic corruption within the Holy Empire, Arantir learns that the time of the Dark Messiah is at hand. He also discovers the mage Menelag, from the free city of Stonehelm, is trying to find the Skull of Shadows and that there is a strong connection between Sar-Elam's relic and Sar-Shazzar's prophecy.

Arantir unifies Heresh and focuses all the Necromancers' resources on preventing the coming of the Dark Messiah. His plan is to destroy the Skull of Shadows, thus releasing the lost fragment of Sar-Elam's soul, and fixing the flaw that weakens the prison-world of Sheogh during the lunar eclipses. It is for him the surest way to counter the prophecy and ensure that the Demons will be eternally locked in Sheogh.

985-989 YSD — MENELAG LOCATES THE SKULL OF SHADOWS

After decades of researching ancient documents long thought destroyed, exploring ancient ruins, and interrogating spirits, the mage Menelag finally locates the Skull of Shadows. It is buried within a ruined Shantiri temple, on a savage and isolated island on the Jade Sea, once deserted, but now inhabited by an Orc tribe who call themselves the "Redskulls" and follow their Shaman, Aratrok.

Menelag convinces the elders of Stonehelm to finance an expedition to Redskull island. Menelag and his crew begin to excavate the temple and its surroundings, harried by the hostile Orcs. After four years of frustration, they finally find the Skull, but it is sealed in an impenetrable crypt. The only way through is to reactivate the magical energies of the temple itself with a Shantiri crystal – a very rare kind of magical gem, one that the Demonist Phenrig, Menelag's secret master, happens to own.

989 YSD — SARETH'S JOURNEY

Phenrig sends his apprentice, Sareth, son of Isabel and Kha-Beleth, on a fateful journey to the city of Stonehelm. The young man, still unaware of his heritage, carries with him the Shantiri crystal that will allow Menelag to gain access to the Skull of Shadows. To guide and protect his charge, Phenrig binds a succubus, Xana, to Sareth's soul.

Sareth arrives at Stonehelm just ahead of an Undead army, led by Arantir himself. The Necromancers manage to infiltrate the city, murder Menelag,

and steal the Shantiri crystal. With Xana urging him on, Sareth tracks the Necromancers and steals back the crystal.

With Leanna, Menelag's niece, he sets sail for Redskull island. Together, they open the crypt containing the Skull of Shadows. Facing the Skull's guardians, Sareth makes his way into the very heart of the tomb. There, he finds the precious relic and takes it, learning all at once his true nature and his true destiny. But Arantir has been chasing them since Stonehelm. He captures Leanna, attacks Sareth, leaving him for dead, and steals the Skull. Brought back to conscience by Xana, Sareth escapes Aratrok's Orcs and sails back to Stonehelm.

Once back in Stonehelm, Sareth finds the chaos of war around him. The Necromancer army has broken into the city, and he must fight his way to the sanctuary where Arantir plans to destroy the Skull. To shatter the relic, Arantir needs a tremendous amount of mystical energies. His solution is to sacrifice the citizens of Stonehelm in a sudden burst of destructive magic and channel their souls into the Skull, to crack it open. But Sareth defeats Arantir before he can complete his ritual...

989 YSD — THE COMING OF THE DARK MESSIAH

Strange signs and portents are seen. On Midsummer's Day, the sun rises blood red and stays that colour all day. The Dwarves' volcanoes are unusually active. Lightning strikes the central tower of the Wizard city of Al-Safir eleven times, an unlucky number. In the Elven Kingdom, the spring flowers all bloom black or blood red. Twin comets appear in the sky, then suddenly vanish. None, not even the Blind Brothers, can interpret the signs, or explain what they mean.

In the world's darkest hour, Sareth holds up the future of Ashan in his hands along with the Skull of Shadows. He must choose whether to embrace his heritage or deny it, whether to hand the Skull over to his father Kha-Beleth and free the Demons from their prison-world, or destroy the relic, and complete Sar-Elam's ritual to seal the Demons in Sheogh for all eternity...

BOOK OF DRAGONS
GODS AND MAGIC

DRAGONS

In the world of Ashan, Dragons are not mere "gigantic winged fire-breathing reptiles," but are Ashan's primordial gods and the embodiment of magic. The natives of Ashan are aware of the Dragons' existence and hold them in respect, if not always in awe. Oaths are sworn on them, and their presence infiltrates everyday conversation.

These days, only the lesser Dragons walk in Ashan. Avatars of the Dragon Gods, they are a pale reflection of their true magnitude and glory. The real Dragon Gods wait in the Spirit Realm, accepting worship and awaiting the day they can return.

THE PRIMORDIAL DRAGONS

ASHA
THE DRAGON OF ORDER

She is the creator goddess, the mother of Time and Space, the triple-faced figure of birth, life and death. She brought the world into existence and then hatched the six Elemental dragons to rule over it.

She controls the fates of all mortal creatures – she spins forth their destiny at birth, measures it through their life, and cuts it at their death. Asha is carefully neutral. She does not show favour to good men or evil men, Dwarves, Elves or Orcs. All of the universe is her creation. However, she is diametrically opposed to the Chaos principle embodied by her insane twin brother Urgash and his demented children, the Demons.

After the Wars of Creation, Asha retired to a safe refuge within the moon, there to sleep, heal and dream. The Moon is in fact the cocoon she wove around herself. It is an image of the Cosmic Egg, a means to measure time, the final resting place of the Dragons and the gate to the Netherworld (where all souls come from and where they all go back after death).

Asha is not worshipped directly. She is above such things. But she is served by the White Weavers, the Blind Brothers, and the Silent Sisters who, throughout the world, help women give birth, perform auguries and supervise funeral rites (thus working as midwives, seers and oracles, embalmers and undertakers).

Note: The Necromancers (*Necropolis faction*) have chosen Asha as their patron-deity. However, their vision of her powers and attributes is twisted, a perversion of her death-dealing nature.

THE THREE FACES OF ASHA

The Mother – LIFE – CREATION – THE PRESENT – GIBBOUS / FULL MOON

The (ever-pregnant) Mother regards all things as her creation and her children. By giving birth, she sets Chaos into form and gives meaning to potential. It was she who spun the first Dragons out of the Void and created the universe, and she continues to encourage it to grow.

She is the "Heart", unconditional love, compassion for all – good and evil.

The Maiden – FATE – BALANCE – THE FUTURE – HALF MOON

The Blind Maiden is Destiny's herald, stitching here and there, unseen, to make sure that all living creatures fulfill their purpose.

She is the "Hands" that can clutch to save or grasp to kill.

The Crone – DEATH – DESTRUCTION – THE PAST – CRESCENT / NEW MOON

The Crone is the image of death. Wizened and old, she snips the thread of life with a sickle held in gnarled fingers.

She is the "Head", serene intellect, gifted with infinite wisdom and omniscient knowledge.

SYMBOLIC ASSOCIATIONS

The Moon

The number 3 (for her three aspects)

The number 8 (a standing 8 is the shape of an hour-glass and measures time, a lying ∞ stands for infinity and measures space)

PHYSICAL DESCRIPTION

Asha is a gigantic winged dragon with graceful and noble forms, as fits the Mother of the Elemental Dragon Gods. Her features are angular rather than rounded, perfectly symmetrical, seemingly complex yet absolutely ordered. Her scales are as black as the void between the stars, but myriad lights constantly blink on her skin, in organized patterns, like microcosmic constellations. Her eyes shine softly with a silvery light but can also burst in blinding flashes like supernovas. Her wings have a huge span that seems almost infinite to the beholder.

URGASH
THE DRAGON OF CHAOS

Urgash is "raw untamed potential", primordial Chaos in its inexhaustible energy and infinite variety of forms. He is ravenous and insatiable, the "dragon-snake that eats its own tail". He is the father of wanton destruction, of frantic mutation, of rampant madness. He is also the progenitor of the Demons.

Urgash is utterly unpredictable. His "logic" defies mortal reason. He can save one day and kill the next, laugh and cry within a matter of seconds, be alternatively cruel and comforting...

He has been long banished to slumber at Sheogh, Ashan's core, but in this prison-world, the Demons linger, and still strive to carry out his desires.

SYMBOLIC ASSOCIATIONS

The number 0 / the circle (the Ouroboros, negation, the primordial Void, but also the Wheel of Fortune, perfection in revolution, stasis in movement, etc.).

PHYSICAL DESCRIPTION

Urgash is a colossal, wingless dragon with twisted, ever-shifting forms. His features are monstrous, dreadful to behold. His thick dark scales seem to be made of molten, boiling metal, their patterns never staying fixed. Bony excrescences (horns, spikes) constantly erupt from his body, to be almost instantly reabsorbed. The blood that flows from these perpetually renewed wounds is a toxic corrosive ooze that consumes everything it comes into contact with. Urgash's body is perpetually surrounded by what seems to be a heat haze that distorts reality. Urgash's mouth is filled with row after row of serrated teeth, and it can stretch to impossible widths. He really is the insatiable Devourer of Worlds.

After centuries of imprisonment in the fiery core of Ashan, Urgash's eyes reflect only pain, madness, hunger, and hatred.

THE ELEMENTAL DRAGONS

MALASSA
THE DRAGON OF DARKNESS

The Dragon of Darkness is the Faceless Foe, the Slithering Shadow with a hundred faces and a thousand whispers. Darkness is a fickle and dangerous master. Darkness may seem meaningless and formless, but she knows. She has always been here and there, watching from close or afar, drinking the words and screams of the mortal races. In her abyssal womb lie all the forgotten memories and the buried secrets of the past.

Malassa is mostly worshipped by madmen and doomsayers, fearless spies and assassins. Malassa holds sway over the shadowy and mysterious **Faceless**, a race almost brought to extinction during the Elder Wars. In the Historical Age, she made a sinister pact with the Dark Elves (*Dungeon faction*).

PHYSICAL DESCRIPTION

Malassa is the most elusive of the Elemental Dragons. Her exact features are impossible to fathom. Her body and wings are covered in black scales, shimmering with a purple hue, but it is semi-immaterial, as if she was made of smoke, or sculpted by plays of light and shadow. On her wings, dozens of "eyes" open to peer at the unseen world and bring back forgotten secrets.

Malassa never speaks, she whispers. Her words are always cryptic, so that only her most devoted worshippers can hope to understand her.

ELRATH
THE DRAGON OF LIGHT

The Dragon of Light is worshipped as the Sun God and the patron of (legitimate) Authority, Truth, Honour and Justice. His servants seek to illuminate dark places, conquer evil, and celebrate individual valour and heroism. Elrath leads the radiant and immortal **Angels**, but they were almost exterminated during the Elder Wars.

In the Historical Age, Elrath became the patron deity of the Holy Empire (*Haven faction*).

PHYSICAL DESCRIPTION

Elrath is the most resplendent of the Elemental Dragons. His features are all about nobility and authority. His elegant scales are of the purest gold, but instead of merely reflecting the light, they literally shine from within. His wings are not scaly, but feathery, like his children the Angels. Elrath has no "Dragon breath", but when his righteous wrath is stirred, his eyes burst into a streak of blinding light.

ARKATH
THE DRAGON OF FIRE

The Dragon of Fire is rash, hasty, and ill-tempered. Selfish and hot-headed, ferocious in combat, he is ruled by his passions and impulses. He is mostly worshipped by thrillseekers, those who see life as a constant struggle and burn it at both ends, but also by those who, like the blacksmiths, shed their sweat and blood as offering to the fire.

Arkath leads the **Dwarves** (*Fortress faction*), grim masters of forge and fire.

GRAPHIC DESCRIPTION

Arkath is the largest of the Elemental Dragons. His features are all about physical power, ferocity and passion. His thick scales are like lava, searing hot and glowing red-gold. His breath is a stream of flames that incinerates everything it engulfs. Arkath favours a bipedal position (standing on his rear legs to dominate his opponents).

SHALASSA
THE DRAGON OF WATER

The Dragon of Water is humble, quiet and secretive. She is the serene mystic, wisest of the Dragons, and her knowledge is only second to her sister Malassa, the Dragon of Shadow, for her watery realm is ripe with forgotten lore and treasure. In all things, she values diplomacy, versatility and adaptability. Yet, if she decides to act, she is swift and indomitable. You cannot hope to win when you are fighting the waves...

Shalassa is worshipped by sailors, fishermen and pirates, but also by prophets, hermits and wisemen. Shalassa peoples her dominion with the reptilian **Nagas** (*Sanctuary faction*), who move freely both in water and on the land.

PHYSICAL DESCRIPTION

Shalassa is the most graceful of the Elemental Dragons. Her features are all about serenity and wisdom. Her scales are a harmonious mix of jade-green and turquoise-blue. Shalassa is wingless and she has fins instead of legs. In fact, she looks like a sea-serpent. Shalassa's breath can be a tidal wave, a geyser of scalding steam, or a bone-chilling blizzard.

SYLANNA

THE DRAGON OF EARTH

The Dragon of Earth is the stolid, slow, even-tempered one among the Elemental Dragons. Peaceful and cautious, Earth acts only after long deliberation and study. She often serves as a peacemaker among her siblings. She is Nature's warden, being very fond of the plants, animals and living rocks that grow "on her back", and the only way to wake her wrath is to destroy or defile her sacred groves and stone circles.

Sylanna is worshipped by druids, rangers, hunters, farmers and herders, and also by wood and stone carvers. Sylanna is beloved of the **Elves** (*Sylvan faction*), silent stewards of her forests.

PHYSICAL DESCRIPTION

Sylanna is the sturdiest of the Elemental Dragons. Her features are all about resilience and quiet determination. Her thick emerald scales are diamond-hard and always covered with moss, plants, trees, etc. Sylanna is wingless, and her legs are massive and short (so that she can be closer to the ground). When angered, she can stomp with them to create tremors. Sylanna's breath is a cloud of mineral shards that can tear their targets to shreds or "petrify" them by covering them whole like a gangue.

YLATH
THE DRAGON OF AIR

Young and impetuous, the Dragon of Air is the seeker of hazardous knowledge, of crafts that are handed down by the shortlived humans from father to child, of myriad facts about the world which he views from on high. Like the wind, he travels everywhere to collect all the sights and sounds he can pick on his way. Curious and intuitive, he is quick to sense the meaning of all things, but he is also restless and frivolous.

Ylath never asked to be worshipped. His only commandment is that his followers should explore, learn, and enjoy all things in life, but mostly, that they should do as they wish, as long as they respect and honour the world that the Dragons created (this point being the crucial line drawn between Ylath and Urgash). As his chosen people, Ylath selected the **Humans**, for they are the youngest race, as he is the youngest dragon, and as curious and restless as he is. But in the Holy Empire, his cult has been supplanted by that of his elder brother Elrath, the Dragon of Light. However, Ylath is still very popular among the nomad barbarian tribes that roam the vast territories stretching beyond the Empire and in the Free Cities.

He is also honoured by the travellers, bards and spies, by the mummers, courtiers, rakes and thieves, and even by some Wizards (for his extensive arcane knowledge but also his tendency to make even the simpler facts appear "hermetic").

PHYSICAL DESCRIPTION:

Ylath is the smallest of the Elemental Dragons. His features are all about speed and agility. His delicate scales are silvery-white. His long wings seem frail, but they are powerful enough to create a whirlwind. Ylath's breath is a bolt of lightning that can strike with accurate precision.

DRAGON MAGIC

SCHOOLS OF MAGIC

Magic is linked to Dragon Gods, and each Magic spell is defined by a School. There are seven Schools of Magic:

- **1 Primordial school**, connected to the Primordial Dragons (Asha – Order, and Urgash – Chaos)
- **6 Elemental schools**, based on the Elemental Dragons (Light, Darkness, Fire, Water, Air, Earth)

THE SCHOOL OF PRIME

Prime Magic comes from Asha or Urgash, the Primordial Dragons, and is connected to the spiritual substance born from the Void. It can channel the magical energies from the spirit world to the material world (and vice versa), and control the space-time continuum (to preserve or disrupt it).

Prime magic can enchant an item (imbue an inert substance with a magical "soul"), animate a Golem or a Skeleton (bind a spirit to a material lifeless form), open a gate between the material and the spiritual world, etc.

Prime Magic is favoured by the worshippers of Asha and the followers of Sar-Elam (the Wizards, the Necromancers, the White Weavers, the Blind Brothers, the Silent Sisters, the Dragon Knights) but also by the servants of Urgash (the Warlocks and Demons).

THE SCHOOL OF AIR

Air Magic comes from Ylath and is linked to the winds, clouds and lightning, but also to intelligence and reason as it is the element of Air that governs the rational mind. It can create a shield of winds to deflect incoming missiles, an air pocket to prevent drowning or suffocation, a lightning bolt to inflict electrical damage, or inspire clarity to dispel confusion and illusions.

Air Magic is favoured by the Humans of the Free Cities and very popular with the Orcs.

THE SCHOOL OF DARKNESS

Dark Magic comes from Malassa and is related to the mysterious, unfathomable shadows, to the subconscious mind, and to the lethargic, and sometimes lethal, powers of sleep, fatigue and coma. Darkness hides and shelters its followers but weakens its enemies and feeds them with intangible horrors or disruptive delusion. It can wrap allies in shadows to help them disappear from view, drain the lifeforce of enemies until they fall unconscious, or conjure their worst nightmares in their mind until they flee in terror or become catatonic.

Dark Magic is favoured by the Faceless and the Dark Elves, and very popular with the Necromancers.

THE SCHOOL OF EARTH

Earth Magic comes from Sylanna and governs the mineral, vegetable and animal kingdoms, involving stone, dust, soil, wood and flesh, but also the feral instincts and the five senses. It is the path that leads to perfect harmony with Nature. It can heal and regenerate what is wounded or weakened, improve the stamina or heighten the senses, remove toxins, poisons, and diseases, but also unleash the powers of nature to turn trees into mighty warriors or cause earthquakes.

Earth Magic is favoured by the Elves and very popular with the Orcs.

THE SCHOOL OF FIRE

Fire Magic comes from Arkath and manifests itself as flames, smoke and ashes. It is also related to the burning passions: desire, courage and anger, lust, recklessness and rage. Fire consumes the weak but gives strength and purpose to the strong. It can create smoke screens and fire shields to protect its allies or fill them with unyielding determination, but it can also incinerate its enemies with scorching fireballs.

Fire Magic is favoured by the Dwarves and very popular with the Demons.

THE SCHOOL OF LIGHT

Light Magic comes from Elrath and is linked to ideals of Truth, Justice, and Perfection. Light shines on the virtuous but blinds and burns the impious. It can heal its servants, even bring them back to life, protect them against various kinds of curses, and pierce through illusions and stealth.

Light Magic is favoured by the Angels and the Priests of the Holy Empire.

THE SCHOOL OF WATER

Water Magic comes from Shalassa and is linked to its various aspects (oceans, lakes, brooks, springs, rain, mist, steam, snow, ice, blood and tears...) but also to emotions, intuition, creativity and empathy.

Water magic renders the body and the mind as malleable as a liquid. It can conjure dream visions, trigger violent emotions but it can also drown armies of enemies in tidal waves or freeze them to death in raging blizzards.

Water Magic is favoured by the Nagas.

"WAYS" OF MAGIC

There are many "paths" to Magic, but the nature of its practice remains the same.

THE PATH OF ELEMENTAL DRAGONS

For the Human Priests of the Light, the Elf Druids, the Dark Elf Sorcerers, the Dwarf Rune Priests, and the Naga Ritualists, Magic equates to Faith. Spells are miracles, granted by the Dragon Gods, through their spiritual servants.

In return for these gifts, the followers of the Elemental Dragons offer their worship. By praying and performing the correct rituals, they willingly channel their own spiritual essence to their Gods.

THE PATH OF SAR-ELAM

The followers of Sar-Elam do not revere the Elemental Dragons as gods, but rather as "Enlightened Beings", Spirits of the highest form and essence, powerful symbols and metaphors for understanding and channelling the powers of Magic. Magic is simply a higher form of knowledge that must be developed through extensive study of arcane lore (mainly the teachings of Sar-Elam) and a rigorous discipline.

Knowledge is a Wizard's true religion. The Wizards believe that they too can achieve the power of the Dragons, as Sar-Elam did before. This can only happen through a lifelong quest for knowledge and an accumulation of power.

Wizards favour understanding and believe in diversity. All life carries knowledge, and the smallest flower or animal might contain wisdom to help understand the whole. This path sometimes leads the Wizards to justify experiments that rationalize the sacrifice of any life in the quest for higher knowledge.

Philosophy on the "perfect path to enlightenment" differs from one faction to another however. The Wizards are "scientists" of magic who value study and experimentation. Instead of praying to the Spirits, they bend them to their will.

The main source of their magic is therefore in the spirits that serve them and the artefacts they create or collect, in which spirits of all magnitude are bound.

The various servants of Asha (White Weavers, Blind Brothers, Silent Sisters) and the Necromancers are more esoteric in their approach to Magic. They have a deep respect for Asha, which is almost religious in nature. They gather in congregations and perform various rituals to honour their Patron-Goddess, even though Asha does not answer prayers, contrary to her Elemental children. For them, Magic is still an object of study, but like a sacred text that only the true believers can decipher.

The Dragon Knights are mystics who preach a direct and intimate contact with the "divine", whom they believe to be an internal, rather than external presence. They are the closest to Sar-Elam's teachings in that they consider that they themselves can achieve the power of the Dragon Gods, as Sar-Elam did before. The main source of their Magic is within themselves. Their artefacts are nothing but an extension of their own inner power.

THE PATH OF CHAOS

The servants of Chaos, Demons and Warlocks, do not really worship Urgash, but they can tap into their Chaos-tainted souls to perform wild Magic, which is essentially destructive and corruptive in nature.

THE PATH OF THE ORC SHAMANS

Because they are a created race, Orcs don't belong to Asha's natural order and have no connection to the Dragon Gods. As a result their magic is not a form of worship of the Dragons and their spirit servants, nor is it a mental discipline based on study and practice, like the Wizards' arcane path. Rather, it is their Demon blood that grants them access to a limited form of Chaos Magic.

Orc Shamans thus use bloodletting rituals to tear the Veil and connect the visible, material world and the invisible spirit world, which they call the "Dream World".

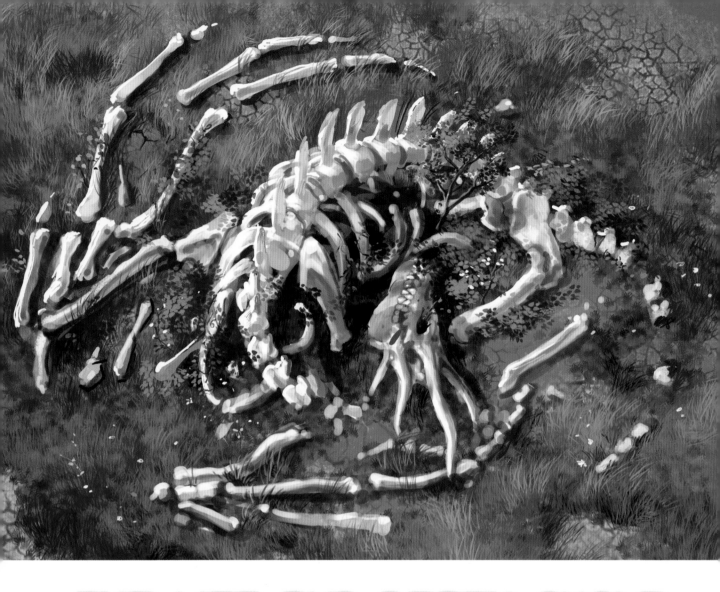

THE LIFE AND DEATH CYCLE

Death was Asha's gift to the countless victims of the Wars of Creation, to terminate their agony and allow them to find peace. But Asha also wanted her soul filled peoples to live a thousand lifetimes, experience a thousand stories. So she transferred their immortal spirits into new bodies, to be reincarnated over and over again, thus creating the cycle of Life and Death. Since that time, when the children of Asha die, they pass into the Void, crossing an invisible barrier between Ashan and the Spirit World, called the Veil. Guided by the silvery light of the Moon, they fly to Asha's resting place, to receive her blessing. Renouncing their mantle of memories, they dive back to Ashan, driven by their sole determination and thirst for passion. With each new rebirth, their desire for understanding is honed anew.

At the time of the new moon, the spirits of the dead are confused as to their final destination, and some linger in the Netherworld, a hole in the fabric of the Veil, a halfway place between the material world and the spirit world.

Urgash did not like the cycle of Life and Death that his sister Asha had created. To his own children, the Demons, he offered a semblance of immortality. Endlessly respawning upon each destruction of their material form – an excruciatingly painful process – the Demons keep their identity and memories, for they do not pass through the Veil. But their newborn body is usually of a lower form and power than the one they've just left.

This explains why a Demon's grudge is eternal. The faces of their enemies are engraved strongly in their minds, never fading, never dissolving.

THE BLOOD OF DRAGONS

During the Wars of Creation, when the Dragon Gods fought against one another, their blood fell over Ashan. It formed a network of Dragon Veins and Nexuses that, with the passing of time, crystallized into magical nodes. These are physical proof that the Dragon Gods once walked the surface of Ashan and flew its skies.

These powerful magical sites became sacred to the Shantiris, elected as places of pilgrimage and meditation, and sometimes founding places of temples or cities. As centuries passed and the Shantiris disappeared, the Dragonblood crystals became more strategic than sacred, for their magical powers could be used to craft powerful weapons and artefacts.

As the crystals were consumed they became rarer, and their value increased even further, until they became the most precious resource on Ashan. The control of a Dragon Vein became synonymous with absolute wealth and power. There are seven different types of Dragonblood crystals, one per Dragon God.

CHAOS SHARD
the Blood of Urgash
Its powers are linked with luck and preternatural insights, but also physical and psychic corruption, mutation and madness.

SHADOW VEIL
the Blood of Malassa
Its properties are linked with the element of Darkness, the mind-numbing and life-draining powers of the Void, but also hallucinations and visions of forbidden knowledge.

BLAZING EYE
the Blood of Elrath
Its properties are linked with the element of Light, with healing and purging, and with the power of True Sight, being able to see through illusions.

SCARLET SPARK
the Blood of Arkath
Its properties are linked with the element of Fire, with the adrenaline rush, physical speed and strength.

EMERALD LEAF
the Blood of Sylanna
Its properties are linked with the element of Earth, with health, stamina and regeneration.

DREAM DROP
the Blood of Shalassa
Its properties are linked with the element of Water, and with the subtle emotions – rapture, melancholy and sorrow.

PRISTINE BREATH
the Blood of Ylath
Its properties are linked with the element of Air and with an improved clarity of mind and alertness of body, including sharpened senses and heightened reflexes.

THE TEARS OF ASHA

The Tears of Asha are highly superior forms of Dragon Crystals. Ten times larger, and a hundred times more powerful than the dragonblood crystals, these extremely rare gems were shed by Asha to end the Wars of Creation and cleanse the corruption and devastation that the forces of Chaos had brought to her creation.

Their powers are nothing short of miraculous, permanently affecting a whole city or region, and capable of bending the laws of Life, Death and Fate themselves.

ARTEFACTS

Artefacts are built-in, magically-sensitive materials (Starsilver, Shadowsteel, Treant wood, Unicorn horn, Moonsilk, etc.). They often have embedded Dragonblood crystals to amplify their power.

Artefacts are commonly used as catalysts by Magic-users to focus their concentration and channel their power. Artefacts can be divided into four categories:

MINOR ARTEFACTS

Minor Artefacts are magical items created by Wizards. They are quite common in Ashan. Even if their purpose is mainly utilitarian and their enchantments are relatively weak, they can make the difference between success and failure, victory and defeat.

MAJOR ARTEFACTS

Major Artefacts are the creations of master craftsmen. They are often unique pieces, created at the request of a wealthy client. They are not only useful, but also beautiful objects. They are much rarer than Minor Artefacts and often found in the possession of nobles and chieftains.

RELIC ARTEFACTS

Relics are items that go beyond the simple crafting of an artisan and enchantment of a Mage. Exposed to a powerful Dragon vein, or generated by an exceptional magical event, they are permanently imbued with powerful magic which will usually change the very nature and shape of the original item.

Relics are well known artefacts, highly sought after and usually very powerful.

LEGENDARY ARTEFACTS

Legendary artefacts are ancient relics of tremendous power associated with renowned heroes from ages past. They are semi-sentient items, inhabited by a Spirit who shares his power with the artefact's owner. The Spirit also acts as a memento of the event that saw the birth of the artefact, and dictates its particular nature and use

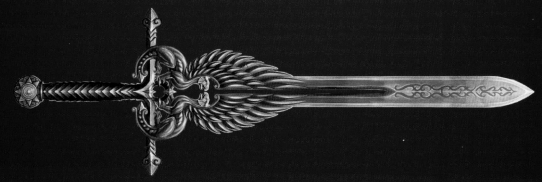

ACADEMY BOOK
THE WIZARD CIRCLE

SUMMARY DESCRIPTION

IN A NUTSHELL

Wizards are proud seekers of knowledge and subjugators of the natural order. They prize knowledge and research above all, and their great weakness is their desire to seek for these things in places – and in ways – that might be best left unexplored. Intellectually competitive, sybaritic, and Machiavellian, others often find them arrogant and supercilious.

Aka: The Wizards, the Mages, the Silver League
Associated Colours: Orange (saffron), gold and azure (mana) blue
Country / Kingdom: The Seven Cities, then the Silver Cities
Capital City: Al-Safir, the Sky Dome

HISTORY

The first kingdom of Wizardry was the confederation of Seven Cities, founded by three disciples of the Seventh Dragon. Located in the southern deserts of Thallan, the Cities were originally intended to be places where the study of magic could be conducted without interruption or distraction. Naturally, however, with power came distraction and dissolution, and the cities descended into decadence. They grew wealthy and populous, and each raised a gemstone tower a thousand feet in the air as a sign of their power.

During the War of the Blood Moon, the Wizards achieved perhaps their greatest hubris, the creation of the Orcs. In the laboratories of Al-Rubit, the Crimson Wizards experimented with Demon blood, which they inoculated into Human slaves and criminals.

The Orc shock troops became the decisive weapon in the conflict, turning its tide and saving Ashan from total destruction. However, once the war was won and the danger passed, a terrible decision was made on the fate of the surviving Orcs. They were resettled as slaves and indentured troops to work the mines and guard dangerous borders in the Seven Cities and the neighbouring Holy Falcon Empire.

Afterwards the Crimson Wizards created the Beastmen by exposing Humans and various animals to powerful Dragon Nexuses, combining them into various hybrid species. The stated purpose of the Beastmen was to replace the Orcs as workers, servants, guards and playthings in the Seven Cities. They were considered slightly superior creatures, because they contained no demon blood.

Bitter at their enslavement, the Orcs and the Beastmen proclaimed their independence from their Wizard masters. The revolt quickly spread to the Holy Empire, leading to the bloody Orc Crusades. To replace their rebellious servants, the Wizards turned to an unexpected source: the Undead.

Belketh was a talented student of Sar-Shazzar who focused his studies of the Revelations of the Seventh Dragon to a fragment dealing with Necromancy, the power of the immortal soul. By gaining control over ghosts and animated corpses, Belketh and his followers could count on endless supplies of ever-obedient servants that knew no fear, had no need to rest or feed, and possessed no desire to rebel. Their philosophy immediately proved popular throughout the Seven Cities.

Eventually the differences between Wizards and Necromancers grew too vast to bridge. Fearing the ever-increasing strength and numbers of the disciples of Belketh, the rulers of the Seven Cities initiated a large-scale persecution, ranging from the seizing of their properties, to banishment, to the spectacle of public executions. That, they thought, would solve the problem. They were wrong. Necromancer sympathizers within the Seven Cities, aided by their exiled allies, launched a revolt.

The Necromancers were finally defeated and forced to settle in the valleys of Heresh. They declared their independence, using the city of Nar-Heresh as their base of operations to plan their revenge. The Wizards, for their part, had to modify the borders of their kingdom. Lamenting their lost "golden age", they named their new home the Silver Cities.

Some of their numbers, disgruntled with the jurisdiction of their peers, chose voluntary exile and left for the trackless wilds. Most sold themselves as rogue mages to the Free Cities. The Crimson Wizards of Al-Rubit and their Beastmen servants, now rejected in favour of the Constructs, settled to the west and founded the city of Karthal on the coast of the Irisus Sea.

On the verge of the fourth Eclipse, the Wizards were arrogant in their power and convinced their enemies were vanquished. Their cities, freed from the Necromancer threat, again asserted their independence, squabbling with one another to the detriment of all. Defences were not repaired, watchfulness was replaced by greed, and the entire nation rapidly made itself utterly unprepared for war.

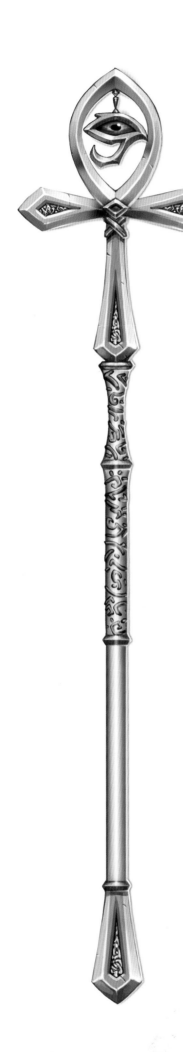

It is that moment that the Necromancers chose to launch a surprise assault. For ten years the conflict raged and the massive waves of destructive magic used by both sides left much of the land uninhabitable.

The once fertile valleys of Heresh were "vitrified", and it became a barren wasteland, filled with bones and laments. The Surviving Necromancers went into hiding. The Wizards were themselves considerably weakened. It took a Wizard of great power to reunite them into a strong nation - one called Cyrus, who would father the legendary Zehir, saviour of Queen Isabel's throne, the Holy Empire, and the whole world of Ashan.

FAMOUS WIZARDS

THE THREE FOUNDERS OF THE SEVEN CITIES

Sar-Shazzar, the most gifted disciple of the Seventh Dragon.
Sar-Issus, who wrote the first principles of Arcane Magic.
Sar-Aggreth, who wrote the first essays on the nature of Djinns and the Spirit world.

NUR

The Djinn Nur is one of those beings that not only wields magic, but is inherently magical. Nur`s battles with Chaos magic across many worlds made her a legendary figure of Wizard lore. When the Seven Cities were still under construction, a perfidious Wizard tricked and captured her in the hope of absorbing her powers and becoming the equal of Sar-Elam. Unable to control this raw magic, the Wizard was instead consumed by it, which ultimately caused the disappearance of his own tower and most of the surrounding city. Centuries later, the Wizard's tower was found, buried beneath the sands of Sahaar. Thanks to a mysterious set of circumstances, Nur's essence was restored, allowing the Djinn to resume her role as a benevolent guardian of the Spirit World.

MAAHIR

In 820 YSD, the League of the Silver Cities were at war with the Necromancers. The Wizard Maahir, a seasoned traveler, was tasked by the Circle with venturing into the heartlands of Heresh to find and defeat Zoltan, right-hand man of Belketh. To prepare for this battle, Maahir forced his body through endless hardships in the belief that exceptional mental endurance goes hand in hand with exceptional physical endurance. This self-imposed training allowed Maahir to defeat his foe, giving the League's armies a crucial advantage in the war. Following his victory, Maahir succeeded to Archmage Yafiah as First of the Circle. He would lead a successful campaign against the Necromancers that would culminate two years later with the defeat of Belketh himself.

CYRUS

Cyrus was destined for greatness. From an early age he showed the combination of natural talent and intense competitive ambition that leaders often possess and was taught in the art of magic by the great Wizard Azh-Rafir. When his master became corrupted by the forces of Chaos, Cyrus was among those who confronted and defeated him. Cyrus eventually became a young and dynamic First of the Circle. However the death of his beloved wife Nadia, who perished while giving birth to their son Zehir, filled his heart with bitterness, and in time he became more known for his cold-hearted and egotistic attitude than for his brilliance. He remained a powerful Wizard nonetheless, destroying the great Lich Sandro in a magic duel. This glorious victory would eventually prove Cyrus's demise, as he was later murdered by Markal, Sandro's vengeful disciple.

ZEHIR

Excitable, headstrong, and energetic are the sorts of words the older Wizards use to describe Zehir. The son of Cyrus and Nadia, he chose to master elemental magic, figuring (correctly) that if he could control beings as fickle and powerful as Elementals he would be well prepared for any magical struggle. Though the title First of the Circle was granted to the young Wizard in the hope of staving off political infighting during a crisis, Zehir would prove a more-than-competent (if occasionally irritating) leader, defeating his father's murderer Markal, uniting the peoples of Ashan against Kha-Beleth, and eventually leading their armies in the fiery bowels of Sheogh itself. A few years later Zehir would also go down in history as the Wizard who finally made peace with the Orcs, then led by Gotai Khan. During a historic summit held in Shahibdiya, old enmities were set aside in favour of an alliance against the demonic usurpers who had seized control of the Holy Empire.

GEOGRAPHIC LOCATION

The Seven Cities were built in the south-western area of Thallan. The local territory is a mix of fertile lowlands rising to dry, rocky heights. The lowlands consist mainly of floodplains, which depend on the spring floods to bring much needed water and nutrients to the soil. The mountains are steep, but not forbiddingly so, and numerous cities and homesteads have been carved out of their slopes. To the south and west, the mountains fade away to the forbidding desert of Sahaar, home originally to Human nomad tribes sworn to Ylath, the

HOLY FALCON EMPIRE

SILVER CITIES

Dragon of Air. It was subsequently shared with bands of marauders who demonstrated very little faith in the Dragon Gods, and later, the Orcs, who brought gods of their own.

To the east, lies the once fertile valley of Heresh, which became a poisoned no man's land after the Wizards unleashed their most destructive magic over the entire region in their attempt to eradicate the Necromancers.

SOCIAL ORGANIZATION

The Circle of Nine, a senate of the most powerful and most ambitious Wizards in the Silver Cities, rules the kingdom. Each member of the Circle represents a city. In theory, the Circle has absolute control over everything from tariffs to military resources to coinage. In reality, each of the cities maintains a greater or lesser degree of independence, and there is much infighting and politicking. Only in times of crisis does the Circle of Nine exert any real authority.

There are several castes in the Wizard's society, by the hierarchic order: the Wizards, the Blademages, the citizens and the merchants, and the servants. At first, the servants were slaves, but they were later replaced by Spirits, Orcs, Beastmen, Undead and Constructs.

The Wizards are divided into three Orders: the Alchemists (House Materia), the Shapers (House Chimera) and the Summoners (House Anima).

PHYSCIAL DESCRIPTION

Theoretically, the Wizards come from all places and all races of Ashan. However, the majority of them are Humans who have settled in the southern deserts for centuries. These "natives" generally have tanned skin, dark eyes and dark hair.

Fashion in the Silver cities is colourful, refined, and well adapted to the arid climate. Wizards are partial to robes and head coverings. Their ranks are distinguished by features such as length, colours, and patterns. Silk and other shimmering cloth is common, as are bright colours and ornate pieces of jewelry. Shades of blue, orange and yellow are favoured. However, for their travel clothes, Wizards mute the colours and use heavier fabrics.

DIPLOMACY

EXTERNAL RELATIONS WITH OTHER FACTIONS

Historical allies: Haven (Knights), and, to a lesser extent, Sylvan (Elves) and Fortress (Dwarves) – they made common cause in the past against the Demon invasions.

Historical enemies: Inferno (Demons - though some Wizards view Chaos as merely another form of magic and have been seduced and corrupted by its servants), Necropolis (Undead - their cult was born in the Seven Cities but they were later persecuted and banned), Stronghold (Orcs - created by the Wizards to be their slaves and bodyguards, they rebelled and won their freedom but they have not forgiven their "creators").

DUNGEON

Constantly evolving and always surprising. You never know what's going to come out of the caverns, or what it will take to drive them right back down.

FORTRESS

Secretive, and hard bargainers. Slow to give up their secrets but quick to find gold, they require much patience to deal with.

NECROPOLIS

Our cursed bastard brethren. We know where they came from and what they serve. We cast them out before and will do so again.

SYLVAN

Long-lived and observant, they make a fascinating source of data and point for comparison.

HAVEN

Dull, but reliable. Good enough neighbours, I suppose, but their view of the world is sometimes a bit narrow, and they tend to act first and ask questions later.

INFERNO

The Seventh Dragon gave his life to imprison them. We must be ever watchful to ensure they never escape again.

STRONGHOLD

Their creation was a necessary evil. They are savages, to be brushed aside if there's something we want in their lands. Until then, they're of no consequence.

SANCTUARY

Enlightenment is found in regarding the world around you, not in regarding yourself. They are wise, and thoughtful, but they too readily mistake mysticism for knowledge. In the end, their affection for one element is far inferior to our mastery of them all.

INTERNAL DISSENSIONS

Magic is taught in academies in the large cities, as hedge wizardry is frowned upon. These academies are formal places where which courses you attend means a great deal about what you will learn, how you learn it, and how the rest of your life will play out. Wizards tend to cluster into "schools" following the teachings of one great Mage or another, and rivalries between schools are fierce.

CULTURE

CORE PHILOSOPHY

"No Gods, no Masters. Knowledge is Power, and Power is Freedom". The universe is a puzzle to be solved, by whatever means necessary.

RELIGION

Knowledge is a Wizard's true religion. Wizards do not view the Elemental Dragons as gods, but rather as the highest form of the spiritual beings. They are either metaphors for understanding and channelling powers, or perhaps real entities that will eventually be comprehended given time. With enough study and experimentation, the Wizards believe that they too can achieve the power of the Dragons, as Sar-Elam did before.

This can only happen through a lifelong quest for knowledge and an accumulation of power. These scientists of magic favour understanding and believe in diversity. All life carries knowledge, and the smallest flower or animal might contain wisdom to help understand the whole. This path sometimes leads the Wizards to justify experiments that rationalize the sacrifice of any life in the quest for higher knowledge.

MAGIC

For all the other factions of Ashan, Magic equates to Faith. Magic powers are granted by the Dragon Gods, through their spiritual servants, to those who offer their worship and perform the correct rituals. Spells are miracles, gifts from the Gods. For the Wizards, however, Magic is simply a higher form of

knowledge that must be developed through extensive study of arcane lore (mainly the teachings of Sar-Elam) and a rigorous discipline.

Instead of praying to the Spirits, Wizards bend them to their will. The main source of their magic is therefore in the spirits that serve them and the artifacts they create or collect, in which spirits of all magnitude are bound. Wizards are masters of all schools of magic with no discrimination. Their search for power and knowledge gives them access to all existing spells and has led them to develop new ways to use and combine them.

ARCHITECTURE

The defining feature of Wizardly architecture is the tower. Tall, slender, and unmarred by windows except at the very top, these structures house the Wizards' laboratories, libraries, and living quarters. Lower levels hold servants, supplies, enchanted creatures, and whatever else is necessary for the Wizards' comfort. Ordinary citizens are forbidden to construct towers, though the wealthy build what are essentially small palaces. The Wizards' most impressive architectural achievement are their flying cities.

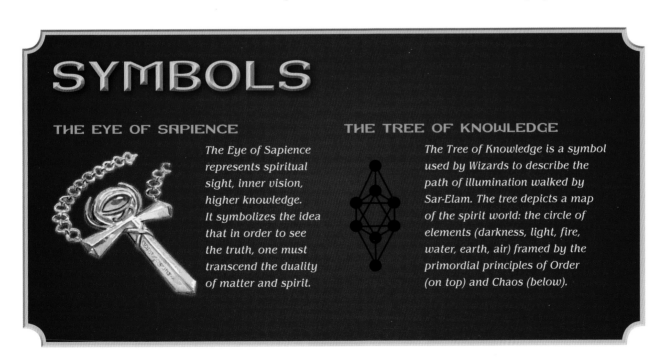

SYMBOLS

THE EYE OF SAPIENCE

The Eye of Sapience represents spiritual sight, inner vision, higher knowledge. It symbolizes the idea that in order to see the truth, one must transcend the duality of matter and spirit.

THE TREE OF KNOWLEDGE

The Tree of Knowledge is a symbol used by Wizards to describe the path of illumination walked by Sar-Elam. The tree depicts a map of the spirit world: the circle of elements (darkness, light, fire, water, earth, air) framed by the primordial principles of Order (on top) and Chaos (below).

WARFARE

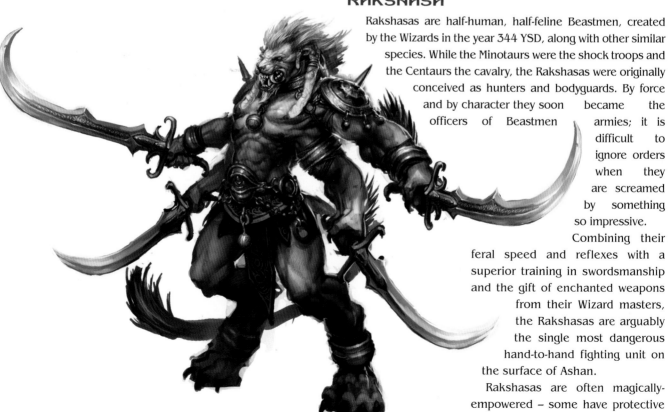

ON THE BATTLEFIELD

Wizards are seen on the front lines about as often as Angels are found in Sheogh, at least if they have anything to say about it. With armies of animated Constructs, Elemental Spirits, and "magically engineered" slave creatures (like the Orcs or the Beastmen) at their beck and call, not to mention "classic" Human troops (often mercenaries), Wizards don't need to get in the middle of the fight.

Constructs like Golems and Titans form the heavy infantry and the core of the Wizards' fighting forces, while Spirits are more equivalent to cavalry in their quick strike capability and power. The strength of these units is that they do exactly what they are told and have no morale issues. Human and "humanoid" shock troops are used to plug breaches, follow up on attacks, and otherwise support the main body of the army.

Wizards stay in the rear echelon, preferably stationed on high ground so they can see and affect the battle without physical risk. They usually serve the role of long-range artillery, launching spells into the fray while staying safely behind the lines.

ICONIC ACADEMY HERO

THE BLADEMAGE

Might and Magic. Sword and Sorcery. This is the Blademage, a mix of a martial and arcane power. The Blademage is a warrior Wizard who channels his spells through his chosen weapon and uses his magic to enhance his ability to strike at his enemies.

ICONIC ACADEMY TROOPS

RAKSHASA

Rakshasas are half-human, half-feline Beastmen, created by the Wizards in the year 344 YSD, along with other similar species. While the Minotaurs were the shock troops and the Centaurs the cavalry, the Rakshasas were originally conceived as hunters and bodyguards. By force and by character they soon became the officers of Beastmen armies; it is difficult to ignore orders when they are screamed by something so impressive.

Combining their feral speed and reflexes with a superior training in swordsmanship and the gift of enchanted weapons from their Wizard masters, the Rakshasas are arguably the single most dangerous hand-to-hand fighting unit on the surface of Ashan.

Rakshasas are often magically-empowered – some have protective

tattoos, others are granted an extra pair of arms. The most powerful are imbued with the essence of ancient Air spirits, making them even more swift and agile. Surprisingly, after the revolt of the Beastmen, many Rakshasas chose to stay with their masters. Having more privileges - as well as being widely feared and respected - was among the main reasons of their unfailing loyalty.

DJINN

When the greatest of all Wizards, Sar-Elam, transformed into the Seventh Dragon, his ascension created a new plane of pure magic in the spirit world. This plane was soon populated by humanoid spirits later called Djinns, and considered to be reflections of the power and brilliance of Sar-Elam. Depending on where, when, and how the Djinn is evoked, it may have a male or a female form (thus perpetuating the ambiguity that surrounds the real appearance and gender of Sar-Elam).

The Djinns are valuable allies for the Wizards, as their mystical knowledge and natural affinity for the currents of magic can strongly influence the scope of a Wizard's abilities.

Whether Djinns collaborate by choice or obligation is determined case by case. In some rare cases, Djinns may voluntarily join with a Wizard because they are intrigued by his research or motivated by his vision. It is more common for Wizards who hunger after the power of a Djinn to try and harness one as a slave; but it is almost as frequent that this act is followed by funeral rites...

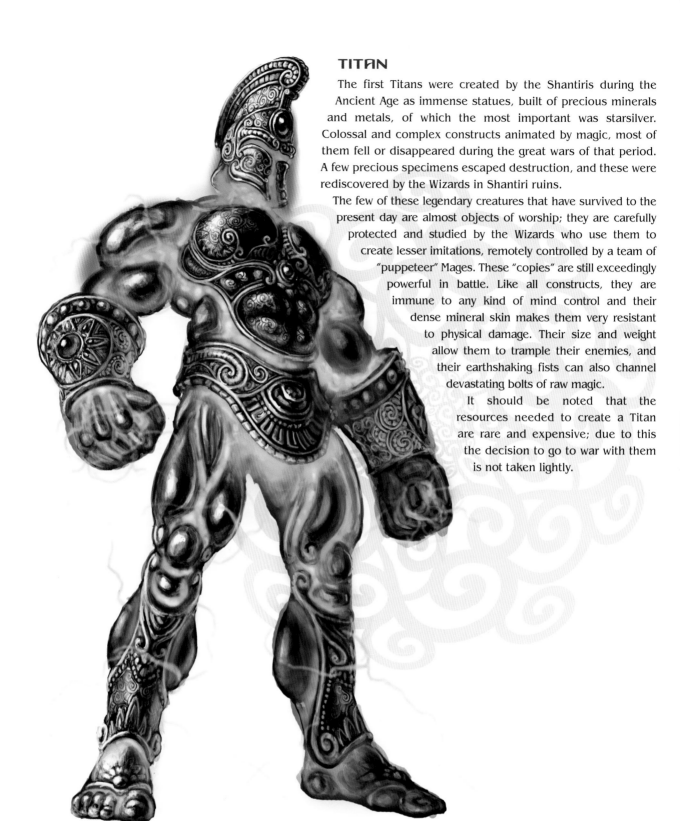

TITAN

The first Titans were created by the Shantiris during the Ancient Age as immense statues, built of precious minerals and metals, of which the most important was starsilver. Colossal and complex constructs animated by magic, most of them fell or disappeared during the great wars of that period. A few precious specimens escaped destruction, and these were rediscovered by the Wizards in Shantiri ruins.

The few of these legendary creatures that have survived to the present day are almost objects of worship; they are carefully protected and studied by the Wizards who use them to create lesser imitations, remotely controlled by a team of "puppeteer" Mages. These "copies" are still exceedingly powerful in battle. Like all constructs, they are immune to any kind of mind control and their dense mineral skin makes them very resistant to physical damage. Their size and weight allow them to trample their enemies, and their earthshaking fists can also channel devastating bolts of raw magic.

It should be noted that the resources needed to create a Titan are rare and expensive; due to this the decision to go to war with them is not taken lightly.

HAVEN BOOK
THE HOLY EMPIRE

SUMMARY DESCRIPTION

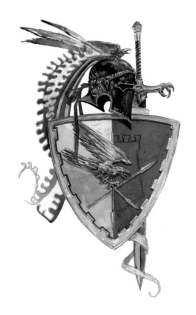

IN A NUTSHELL

The Holy Empire is a theocracy protected by medieval knights and monks. They worship Elrath, the Dragon God of Light, who grants them magical powers based on his elemental dominion. Their objective is to lead a life worthy of Elrath's ideals of Truth and Purity, to shape the world in his image, and to spread his sacred Light.

Aka: The Knights of the Light

Associated Colours: Azure blue, white and gold

Country / Kingdom: The Holy Empire

Capital City: Falcon's Reach, then Talonguard

HISTORY

The Holy Empire was originally a series of squabbling clans. Ronan the Great, High King of the Falcon, united them through a combination of dazzling generalship, brilliant negotiation, and the occasional political marriage. Once the country was under his thumb, he declared the foundation of the Falcon Empire and settled in to make his position as Emperor hereditary. The legitimacy of his claim was supported by the intervention of Sar-Elam, the Seventh Dragon, who blessed the new monarch and prophesied that the Falcon line shall endure as long as the world did.

At about the same time, the Angels were in a dire predicament: their numbers had been declining for centuries because of their courageous but often deadly fighting during the Wars of Creation and the Elder Wars, and their low rate of reproduction.

THE ANGEL SWORDS OF VIRTUE

At the end of the Ancient Age, the Angels had declined in numbers due to centuries of courageous battles in wars with both the Demons and the Faceless. In order to ensure that Elrath, the Dragon God of Light, would continue to have followers, the Angels came up with a plan to convert the newborn Human Empire from its worship of Ylath, the Dragon God of Air.

The Angels' first major action was to persuade the young Emperor Brian Falcon. They forged seven enchanted swords, each named after a virtue of Elrath, giving the most powerful to Brian, and the six others to his most powerful vassals, the dukes of the Realm.

The Duke of Griffin, Ishtvan, was wary of the Angels and their religious meddling. He placed the gift sword over his mantle and never touched it again. But to honour his word of fealty to Brian, he had another sword, Iron Feather, forged.

Ishtvan never wielded the sword in battle as he was murdered shortly after it was completed.

Since his heirs were more respectful of imperial authority and preferred to use the Angel-made sword, Iron Feather was given instead to the cadet children of the Griffin family.

Even if the blade has served the Empire without fault throughout the centuries, it remains a symbol of defiance.

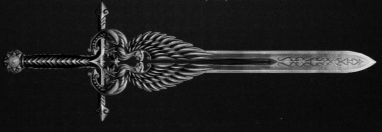

They were facing the end of their race, and consequently, an end to the worship of their patron Dragon-God, Elrath.

So they searched for nations to convert, and they set their eyes on the Humans of the young Falcon Empire, lost in the religious upheaval that had followed Sar-Elam's ascension to Dragonhood and the Wars of Fire.

The Angels approached the young boy Brian, great-grandson to Ronan Falcon, and helped him convert his fragile Empire, forlorn by the fickle Dragon of Air, into a strong nation dedicated to the stern and unforgiving Dragon of Light.

During the First Eclipse, Demons returned to the world of Ashan. The Wizards created the Orcs to stop them. At the end of the invasion, the Orcs were resettled as slaves and indentured troops to work the mines and guard dangerous borders in the Seven Cities and the neighbouring Holy Falcon Empire. After more than a century of oppression, the long-restive Orc population rose up against its creators. They declared themselves free of their masters and of the Dragon Gods, unwilling to kneel in obedience or worship.

This blasphemy could not be born, and the Empire's retaliation was swift. Emperor Connor I declared a holy crusade against the Orcs. For about thirty years, Imperial armies relentlessly drove the Orcs back. A great armada was prepared to sail for the Pao islands on the Jade Sea, with the declared intent to capture or exterminate the local Orc population, to the last child.

But a magical storm of tremendous magnitude arose and sunk the imperial fleet. This, the Emperor decided, was a sign from the Dragons. Enough had been done. The Crusade was over.

Peace, more or less, settled in for two and a half centuries, until the Falcon line was slaughtered by Demon assassins. Before being murdered, Lady Maeve Falcon managed to send her son Brendan to safety, but at the cost of secrecy and the resignation of his claim to the throne.

A gruesome civil war surged across the land, as the various noble houses sought to claim the bloody crown. Eventually, Duke Ivan of the Griffin took the throne by acclamation, and the Empire was renamed the Holy Griffin Empire. The Griffin dynasty ruled unchallenged for two centuries until the Sixth Eclipse and Queen Isabel's war. The death of the last Griffin heir left the throne vacant, and the young Duchess Freyda of the Unicorn was crowned Empress.

GEOGRAPHIC LOCATION

Since its creation, the Empire has been broken up into seven regions. The imperial capital is in the centre, surrounded by six Duchies, each with their own distinct character.

Most of the Empire is made up of rich farmland and rolling hills. The countryside is well watered, with several large rivers snaking across the landscape. To the north, the land rises up to a range of mountains. Older, lower mountains are prominent in the southwest.

SOCIAL ORGANIZATION

The Holy Empire is a theocracy with a feudal structure. In theory the Holy Emperor has absolute rule, but in reality the land is chopped up into six Duchies and countless baronies, so that much of the Emperor's time is spent juggling his various nobles. Frequently at least one of these regions is in some sort of revolt, though these are rarely serious or bloody. The Church of Elrath wields considerable political force, and even the smallest villages have a church near their centre. Priests are allowed to marry, though not actively encouraged to do so.

Angels don't have official roles within the Empire, except in times of crisis when they can get temporary assignments. Most of the time, they act as advisors and counsellors with lofty, but honorary positions.

Knights come from the ranks of nobles and socially ambitious merchants. The rise of the middle class has taken place mostly in the cities, and many of the newly rich traders are seeking to ally their families with noble houses, generally through marriage.

Most peasants don't care who's in charge. They just want to go about their lives, which makes things easier for everyone.

PHYSICAL DESCRIPTION

HUMANS

Humans of the Holy Empire cover the gamut, depending on which region of the Empire they hail from. Northern humans are tall, thin and pale, with light hair. Further south, both skin and hair gets darker. Both men and women wear their hair long. Imperial fashion is very modest, nobles and commoners alike wear clothing that covers as much of their skin as possible. Standard clothing includes tunics and leather jerkins, leggings, and boots. Women often wear dresses with long sleeves and high necklines.

ANGELS

Physically imposing and striking in their perfection, the Angels are taller than normal Humans, generally between six and eight feet tall, with weapons and armour sized to match. They have perfect proportions and project an aura of power and confidence. They sport one or several pairs of large, strong feathered wings on their back. Their skin can be of any tone, but always radiates a soft golden halo. Their eyes are gold and as bright as the Light of their patron god, Elrath.

RACIAL ABILITIES

Being Elrath's devoted servitors, the Angels naturally cling to the image and ideals of the Dragon of Light. In return for their unconditional worship, they are blessed with a natural affinity for Light magic.

Angels also have a unique aura that covers their faces and alters them slightly, so as to look more like the people who observe them. An Elf would see them as slightly Elven, an Orc would give them Orcish traits, etc. In any case, Angels are uniformly beautiful to the eye of their audience, always matching their highest aesthetic canons and looking eternally young.

DIPLOMACY

EXTERNAL RELATIONS WITH OTHER FACTIONS

Historical allies: Academy (Wizards), Sylvan (Elves), Fortress (Dwarves) - all have allied with the Empire in the past against the Demon invasions.

Historical enemies: Inferno (Demons - Haven's nemesis since the first days of the Empire), Necropolis (the Undead - their cult was purged by the Church of the Light), Stronghold (Orcs - they were once slaves of the Empire, and they rebelled), Dungeon (Dark Elves - not really enemies but branded as such by the Church of Light because they worship Malassa, the Dragon of Darkness).

ACADEMY

The Wizards are courteous allies and noble trading partners, even if their observance is a bit... lacking. They will no doubt come to see the error of their ways.

DUNGEON

Disgusting. Who knows what foul rites they perpetrate down in their dark warrens, or what vile things they worship?

FORTRESS

At times, they have done their part against the Demons. At times, they have not. It is drawing near the time when they must make a stand.

INFERNO

Our mortal, sworn enemies. Cursed be he who has dealings with Demons, cursed be he who does not stand up to oppose them.

NECROPOLIS

If half the things I hear of their ways are true, then there's no place for their kind in this world. The consecrated dead should remain dead.

STRONGHOLD

Stronghold? A place of weakness, if you ask me, lands to which cowards retreated in the face of righteousness. When the hour comes, we shall finish the work started so many centuries ago.

SYLVAN

The Elves make strong allies, but there is a savage heart beating in the dark places of the forest.

SANCTUARY

An unnatural way to live for an unnatural people. They hide in deep water because they fear the Light. They are polite and formal enough, but fine manners can hide foul thoughts.

INTERNAL DISSENSIONS

The Holy Empire has known numerous dissensions amongst its six major duchies and hundreds of baronies since the day it converted from Ylath, the Dragon God of Air, to Elrath, the Dragon God of Light.

Though religious disputes are by no means the most common reason for internecine conflict, they have been known to be the most bloody.

Political rivalries over land and the emperor's favour have set the stage for forced marriages and trade embargos. The Holy Emperors have learned how to use this internal tension between the duchies to expand their dominion over the centuries.

It is easily arguable that without a common enemy, the Holy Empire would have dissolved and returned to a mass of scattered clans, in constant conflict with each other, rather than fighting for a common cause. It is thus ironically fortunate that the Empire's history was bloodied by countless conflicts with the Demons, Elves, Orcs, Necromancers and various border skirmishes with the Free Cities. This semi-permanent state of martial law has allowed the Inquisition to keep the empire mobilized for war for several decades.

ON THE ART OF RUSE

Anton: *We need to find a way to open the gates.*

Jezebeth : *If we could slither, we could dress up like Nagas?*

Kilburn: *Lady Jezebeth... As soldiers of Elrath we despise trickery.*

Jezebeth: *Actually, we're just not very good at it.*

ON THE AGE OF ANGELS

Laurielle: *In my twenty-three centuries of loyal service to Elrath, I haven't seen anyone use a siege engine so well since the Demon Azkaal destroyed the sky city where I was born.*

Jezebeth: *How old did you say you were?*

Valeska: *Lady Jezebeth... it's never polite to remind a woman of her age.*

CULTURE

CORE PHILOSOPHY

"Law & Order" rather than "Good & Mercy"

Driven by the Angels, Elrath's chosen, the children of the Holy Empire believe in the flawed nature of the self, which must be cleansed in the light of Elrath. Their objective is to lead a life worthy of Elrath's forgiveness, shape the world in his image and spread his sacred Light.

RELIGION

The Holy Empire is mostly composed of Humans who have switched their allegiance from Ylath, the Dragon of Air, to Elrath, the Dragon of Light. With the Angels mostly gone, the Holy Empire is the primary remaining base of worship for Elrath.

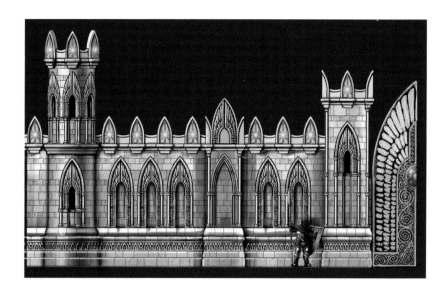

MAGIC

Supported by the few Angels remaining, the citizens of the Holy Empire pray to Elrath in exchange for blessings and miracles. In this system of belief, magic power is proportional to faith. Angels are a bit different. Being an elder race directly related to Elrath, they have an innate affinity with Light magic and its principles of Truth, Justice, and Perfection.

ARCHITECTURE

Imperial architecture is heavy and ornate. Every inch is covered in sculpture, statues, and the like. Stone is the preferred building material, with white marble to cover the outer faces of the holy buildings. Most cities are built around a central castle and keep, and the noble houses generally have protective walls and at least one defensive tower.

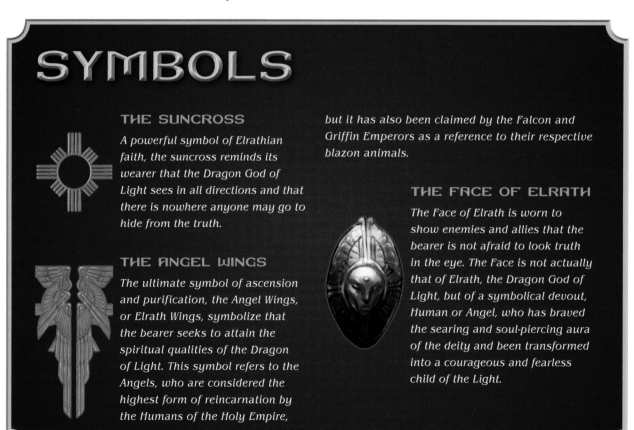

SYMBOLS

THE SUNCROSS

A powerful symbol of Elrathian faith, the suncross reminds its wearer that the Dragon God of Light sees in all directions and that there is nowhere anyone may go to hide from the truth.

THE ANGEL WINGS

The ultimate symbol of ascension and purification, the Angel Wings, or Elrath Wings, symbolize that the bearer seeks to attain the spiritual qualities of the Dragon of Light. This symbol refers to the Angels, who are considered the highest form of reincarnation by the Humans of the Holy Empire, *but it has also been claimed by the Falcon and Griffin Emperors as a reference to their respective blazon animals.*

THE FACE OF ELRATH

The Face of Elrath is worn to show enemies and allies that the bearer is not afraid to look truth in the eye. The Face is not actually that of Elrath, the Dragon God of Light, but of a symbolical devout, Human or Angel, who has braved the searing and soul-piercing aura of the deity and been transformed into a courageous and fearless child of the Light.

WARFARE

ON THE BATTLEFIELD

Mounted knights make up the Empire's heavy shock troops, supported by heavy infantry (the Sentinels, renowned for their discipline and military coordination) and missile weapons (the justly feared crossbowmen).

Each noble is responsible for raising, outfitting and training his local militia and men-at-arms. The entire army is under the command of whichever noble the Emperor has appointed to the post. In theory, anyone is eligible. In practice, very few are ever given command of an army – the Emperor simply doesn't trust many of his vassals with that kind of power.

ICONIC HAVEN HERO

PALADIN

Champions of the impossible quests with faith as their guiding star, Paladins have answered the calling of Elrath, the Dragon God of Light. They have sworn a solemn oath to uphold the principles of their god, and to defend the realm from all enemies. Their vow is magically binding and blesses them with tremendous powers. For this reason, Paladins become a guiding light, honoured by the people, respected by their allies and feared by their enemies.

ICONIC HAVEN ALLIES

GRIFFIN

Griffins were created in the Mythic Age from the spontaneous magical fusion of lions and eagles. At that time the surface of Ashan was irrigated by Dragon veins, remnants of the Dragon Gods' wars, and animals that drank of these untamed rivers of Dragon blood and magic were permanently altered by it. It is said that an act of compassion by an eagle who rescued a lion being carried away by the current of a dragon-vein gave rise to this formidable species.

In the days before the wars between the Elves of Irollan and the Holy Empire, Elf smiths were said to have been so impressed by the harmonious bonds Humans had forged with Griffins, that they taught them the secrets of Starsilver. This metal is as strong as it is light, and when properly crafted makes extremely effective armour for the flying beasts.

The mysterious Elven glyphs found on the bardings of the Imperial Griffins are remnants of that long forgotten friendship.

DIRE WOLF

In the Holy Empire, Dire Wolves are among the most feared predators of the wild. The ruthless warriors of the Wolf Duchy have chosen this bloodthirsty beast as their blazon animal, and they have learned to train them into efficient, if somewhat unreliable, companions for their hunting parties, and of course, for war.

RADIANT GLORY

Vessels of the will of Elrath, the Dragon God of Light, Radiant Glories are shining spirits who can flare into brilliance and blind their enemies.

In the Spirit Realm, Elrath's dominion is filled with myriads of these creatures. They are often sent as envoys and advisors to Elrath's most faithful followers. The generals of the Holy Empire soon found a use for these beings of burning light.

STRONGHOLD BOOK
THE ORC TRIBES

SUMMARY DESCRIPTION

IN A NUTSHELL

Tribes of nomadic barbarians, Orcs are the scattered but proud survivors of a long history of persecution. They boast ranks of fierce warriors supported by powerful Shamans. Their "blood magic", chaotic in nature and linked to their Demon origins, and their shamanistic spells, powered by their link to their ancestors, are limited but devastating when coupled with their relentless resolve.

Aka: The Orcs, the Half-Demons.

Associated Colours: Blood-red and Brown

Country / Kingdom: The Steppes of Ranaar (north-east), the Desert of Sahaar (south-west), and the Pao Islands (south-east).

Capital City: None (nomadic lifestyle)

ORC CUISINE

Contrary to popular belief, Orcs are not cannibals. Their diet is based heavily on the principle of "you caught it, you cook it". Hunting provides the bulk of their diet, and throughout the day a steady stream of Orc hunters will bring their prizes into the camp and prepare them for the community cook fire. Gatherers will add various roots and berries to the daily meals, which is often accompanied by fermented fruit or milk, their beverage of choice.

HISTORY

The Orcs were created in the Seven Cities during the War of the Blood Moon. It is in the laboratories of Al-Rubit that the Crimson Wizards experimented with Demon blood, which they inoculated into Human slaves and criminals. The Orc shock troops became the decisive weapon in the conflict, turning its tide and saving Ashan from total destruction.

However, once the war was won and the danger passed, a terrible decision was made on the fate of the surviving Orcs. They were resettled as slaves and indentured troops to work the mines and guard dangerous borders in the Seven Cities and the neighbouring Holy Falcon Empire. Persecuted and feared, never truly accepted, they grew bitter and resentful towards those whom they saw as the favoured children of the Dragon-gods.

Their resentment finally exploded, and the Orcs rose up against their creators. Born in Shahibdiya, the rebellion, led by the legendary Kunyak, quickly spread to the whole of the Seven Cities and to the Holy Falcon Empire. The Orcs declared themselves free of their masters and of the Dragon Gods, unwilling to kneel in obedience or worship. This blasphemy could not be borne by the Holy Empire, and its retaliation was swift. The Falcon Emperor Connor declared a holy crusade against the Orc heretics.

Though the Orcs and their allied Beastmen fought fiercely, they lost ground until, finally, they had no choice but to flee to the most inhospitable reaches of the world. Once settled in their new territories, they tamed the wild beasts, raided or traded with neighbouring tribes, and slowly developed a common culture based on the values of pride, courage and independence.

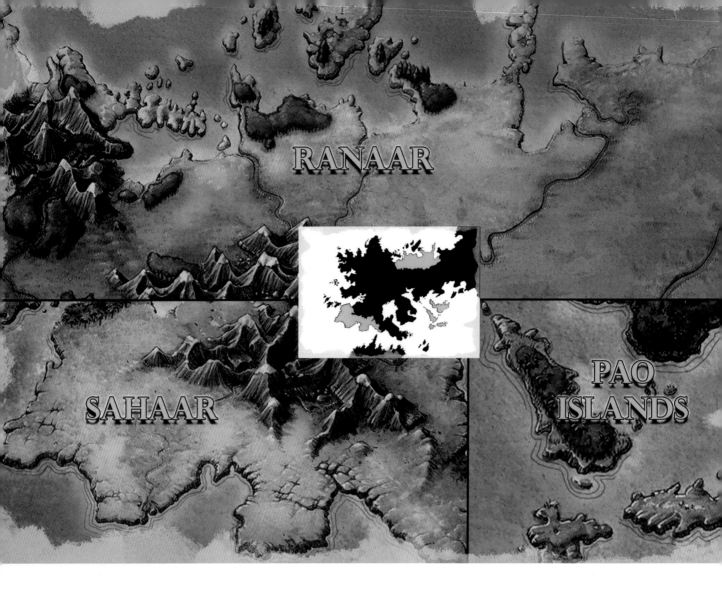

RANAAR

SAHAAR

PAO
ISLANDS

GEOGRAPHIC LOCATION

The Orcs made their new homes in places too harsh for the other races of Ashan. No one has yet mapped the full extent of their wilderness territories, and those who have attempted to do so seldom return. After the Orc rebellion, some went south-east to the Pao Islands, pursued by the crusaders of the Holy Falcon Empire. Others vanished into the forbidding steppes of Ranaar, and enough survived and adapted to form a powerful nation. A third group left the Seven Cities to lead a nomadic life in the dunes of the Sahaar desert.

Orcs rarely settle for long in one particular place, nor would they live underground. They prefer open skies and the freedom to move on when the urge takes them. Occasionally a chieftain puts together a permanent settlement, but this is viewed as an invitation for raiding bands to come and tear it down. As the Orcs love a good fight, this act of bravado seems to please both parties.

SOCIAL ORGANIZATION

Orcs have a tribal organization. Each family group has its own herd or hunting grounds, and either follows the herd or changes hunting grounds with the seasons. Each tribe also has a chieftain and a Shaman, who handle the physical and spiritual needs of the tribe. Marriages between tribes are common, as are short, violent conflicts over real or perceived slights to honour. If a major threat menaces the Orcs as a whole, however, intertribal squabbles are quickly forgotten, and any invaders are faced with a unified front of fierce warriors.

PHSCICAL DESCRIPTION

From their Human origins, Orcs have retained a humanoid form, dexterous hands, and expressive facial features. Some among them (most often females) have slender builds and appealing faces. Most Orcs, however, have been horribly mutated by the chaotic blood that flows in their veins. Thick brown-red skin, hunched shoulders, strong jaws, horns and claws are some of the demonic features that the Orcs have inherited. What they lost in grace and beauty, however, they make up for in strength and resilience. The average male Orc is between six and a half and seven feet tall, and far stronger and tougher than the sturdiest Human warrior.

RACIAL ABILITIES

Because they do not truly belong to Ashan's original design, Orcs are not subject to some of its laws. The most obvious example is Magic, which simply fails more often than not when in contact with an Orc. (This works both ways: Orcs are nearly immune to magic, but also use it poorly and have troubles employing magical artifacts). Orcs are especially resistant to Demon magic. Their skin is practically fireproof, their spirit is immune to demonic possession and many other forms of mind control, and they cannot be duped by illusory magic. These powers made them the ideal shock-troops against the Demons in the past, but they come with a steep price. When their demonic blood gets the better of them, the Orcs fall under the influence of the Bloodrage, a fit of frenzy that drives them to attack everything that crosses their path, both friend and foe. In this altered state the Orcs become insensitive to pain, fight with wild unrestrained aggression and lose all sense of self-preservation.

GOBLINS

Not all of the Wizards' efforts to create the perfect army of warriors were successful. Goblins are "degenerate" Orcs, born from the blood of lesser demons (mostly Imps). The resulting race was considered a failure. As their fertility is inversely proportional to their physical and intellectual capacities, they have multiplied like rodents.

Goblins are smaller than Dwarves (between 4 and 5 feet tall), scraggy, physically weak, but very swift and agile. They have the same brown-red skin and racial abilities as the Orcs.

CYCLOPES

Cyclopes are the Goblins' opposites. They too were a failure in the Orc experiment, but because they were born from the blood of major Demons. The Demon part of their blood took over, and they became monstrous giants, body and mind twisted by chaotic surges.

Cyclops, often over 8 feet tall, look more demonic than Human. A curious trait they all share is that they have only one eye: a large, pupiless disc, red and glowing. No one knows for sure the cause of this mutation, but a popular Wizard theory claims that it is the "Mark of Chaos", a symbol of the Dragon-snake Urgash, coiled in circle, eating its own tail.

DIPLOMACY

EXTERNAL RELATIONS WITH OTHER FACTIONS

Historical allies: none

Historical enemies: Inferno (Demons, the Orcs were bred to fight them, and the Demons did everything in their power to earn the Orcs' enmity), Haven (Knights) and Academy (Wizards) - who were their former enslavers.

INFERNO

Orcs smell Demon blood a hundred leagues away. Find Demons. Kill Demons. Orcs never forget....

HAVEN

Fat steel lords forget that Orcs are not slaves. Orcs are free. When Orcs show teeth, Knights run like sheep. Bah!

ACADEMY

Sometimes Wizards come to "study" Orcs. Orcs burn books and break fingers. Study that! Ha ha haaa!

NECROPOLIS

Dead flesh smells bad. Frightens prey. If Dark Wizards touch Orc dead, Orcs smash them. Stinky Wizards go home.

FORTRESS

Dwarves are like turtles. Hide behind armor shells and bite with steel beaks.

Dwarves make the best blades. Better to see them in marketplace than on a battlefield.

SYLVAN

Elves honor Mother Earth. Druids much like Shamans. Are good warriors, but think too much. Elf talks before battle. Orc talks after.

DUNGEON

Dark Elves are treacherous. Don't talk like Elves. Think fast and act with no words. Better to kill Dark Elf quick and keep eye on shadows.

SANCTUARY

Nagas talk peace but show no fear in battle. Like Orcs, Nagas fight with honor. Better to fight Nagas far from water.

INTERNAL DISSENSIONS

The Orcs' sense of solidarity is built more on the hatred of common enemies than on any unifying principles. They are steadfast in their hatred of the Demons, for instance, and will quickly join together against any force that threatens a family, clan, or tribe. Their sense of existing outside the natural order has given them strong fraternal bonds, so that even Orcs from very different regions of Ashan will feel a certain kinship. Their way of life encourages this, as families and tribes that share pasturage or fishing grounds often come into contact. Songs and tales are shared, and contests of martial skills are common. However, given their choleric nature, fights and bloodshed are as common as laughter and cheering. In fact, when no outside threats are looming, disputes over hunting grounds, mates, and even poorly told jokes can turn the Orcs into their own worst enemies. Clans that share dwindling supplies on the steppes of Ranaar during the harsh winters might easily spill blood the following summer over access to water. There is a saying that an Orc will hold a grudge as long as the sea holds water.

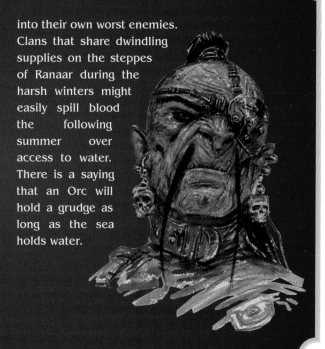

CONVERSATION BETWEEN SANDOR AND KRAAL

Sandor: *How do you say, "Attack!"*

Kraal: *Drava.*

Sandor: *How do you say, "Advance!"*

Kraal: *Drava.*

Sandor: *"Hold your position?"*

Kraal: *Drava.*

Sandor: *"Retreat?"*

Kraal: *Hmmm. Maybe... "Gurr-DA!"*

Sandor: *That sounds pretty aggressive for "Retreat"...*

Kraal: *Nnn. Actually means, "Die where you stand." But is only battle order that doesn't mean "Attack!"*

Sandor: *How do you say: "You know him?"*

Kraal: *Bava.*

Sandor: *That's all? How do you say "I know you."*

Kraal: *Bava.*

Sandor: *Yeah. Okay. How about, "We know them?" "She knows us?" "They know him?"*

Kraal: *Bava. Bava. Bava.*

Sandor: *Uh...*

Kraal: *Orcs don't like pronouns. Heh heh heh.*

CULTURE

CORE PHILOSOPHY

"Never again". This is our home. Your kind is not welcome here. We have made this place our own. No one shall take it from us, and no one shall ever tell us what to do again.

RELIGION

The Orcs have no god. The Orcs need no god. This being said, their Shamans pay homage to Mother Earth and Father Sky, two powerful spirits they meet when they travel into the "Dream World". Sages of other factions have compared these spirits to Ylath and Sylanna (the Dragon Gods of Air and Earth), or to various aspects of Asha.

MAGIC

As they were created then enslaved by the Wizards, Orcs generally hate magic. But they are not stupid. They know that magic is real, and that there are many connections between the visible, material world and the invisible spirit world. Because they are a created race, Orcs don't belong to Asha's natural order and have no connection to the Dragon Gods. As a result their magic is not a form of worship of the Dragons and their spirit servants, nor is it a mental discipline based on study and practice, like the Wizards' arcane path. Rather, it is their Demon blood that grants them access to a limited form of Chaos Magic.

Orc Shamans use bloodletting rituals, and to conjure the more powerful spells they require other Orcs or Goblins to join them. Sometimes they don't ask approval from the participants, and sometimes, they need so much blood that they have to bleed their co-ritualists dry...

ARCHITECTURE

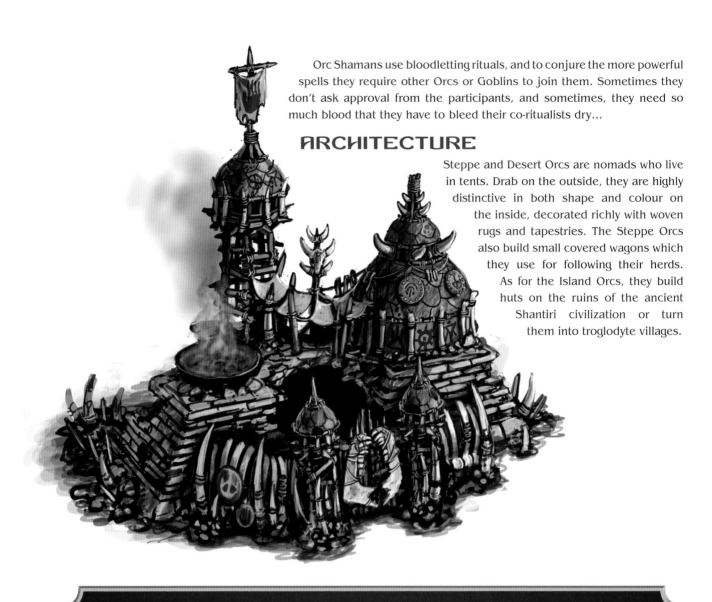

Steppe and Desert Orcs are nomads who live in tents. Drab on the outside, they are highly distinctive in both shape and colour on the inside, decorated richly with woven rugs and tapestries. The Steppe Orcs also build small covered wagons which they use for following their herds. As for the Island Orcs, they build huts on the ruins of the ancient Shantiri civilization or turn them into troglodyte villages.

SYMBOLS

THE BLOODY RED HAND

This is a rich symbol with multiple layers of meaning. It refers to the Demon blood that flows in the Orcs' veins and to the fact that they were created to be the "hands" of the Wizards. Above all, it says that they will never be slaves again. The hand's gesture means, "No more".

FATHER SKY

Father Sky is the power of the Orc clans. He is anger, action, war, and triumph. From the sky comes rain, wind, lightning and thunder. Orc warriors call to these elemental forces before battle and revel in their raw brute energy.

Shamans of Father Sky perform battle blessings, weather magic, auguries and divination. When the clan teeters at the edge of a major conflict the Shamans of Father Sky will always vote for war.

MOTHER EARTH

Mother Earth is the protector and healer of the Orc clans. She is stoicism, contemplation, peace, and community. From the earth comes life and sustenance. Shamans of Mother Earth perform healing rites and a variety of other functions such as leading sacrifices. They also preserve Orc traditions through storytelling and songs. In difficult times, Shamans of Mother Earth think more of the future of the tribe than of the glory of its individuals.

WARFARE

ON THE BATTLEFIELD

Orcs were created as shock-troops to fight Demons, and their tactics reflect this. Orc warriors are mobile, lightly armoured and heavily armed. They usually rush straight at the enemy, counting on their numbers, speed, ferocity and toughness to break the lines of the opposing army without suffering too many casualties. Steppe and Desert Orcs are nomad warriors, born in the saddle, and they train their mounts (aurochs, dire wolves, giant hyenas…) for battle. Some can even ride more exotic creatures, like Manticores or Wyverns. By the same token, it's hard to make the Orcs stand and fight. With no cities to defend, they can retreat endlessly into their native steppes, deserts or jungles and wait for the right moment to counter-attack. Their mobility makes them hard to pin down, and their ability to live off the land makes it impossible to cut off their supply lines. Orcs fight to win but they have developed a "code of honor" that they use when they face a "respectable" enemy (Demons or Wizards are automatically excluded from this category).

ICONIC STRONGHOLD HERO:

THE SHAMAN

Orc Shamans are a strange breed. They act as mediums between the material world and the spirit world, which they refer to as the "Dream World". To enter this realm, they undergo deep trance rituals, the nature of which is specific to each Shaman.

From their journeys into the "Dream World", the Shamans bring insights that help them draw magical powers from their own demon blood.

ICONIC STRONGHOLD ALLIES

CENTAUR

Centaurs are one of the many species created by the Wizards of the Seven Cities. Half-human and half-horse, they served their masters honorably as scouts and mobile archers in their armies. But those days came to an end when the Wizards replaced them with their new creations, the animated constructs. The various Golems, Gargoyles, Titans, etc. were simpler to manage, cheaper to keep, and unfailingly obedient. The Centaurs were given less and less noble tasks, and ended up carrying messages and pulling carts. Disgruntled at their loss of prestige, they willingly joined the Beastmen and scattered across the face of Ashan seeking space, dignity, and freedom.

THE BEASTMEN

Orcs are not the only results of the Seven Cities' experimentation. Around the same time, excited by the success of their creations, the Wizards began experimenting in other ways as well. In combining Humans with different animals, they created many of the species that we now call the Beastmen. Minotaurs, Centaurs and Harpies are among the beings created as servants, playthings and guards for their masters. Most of these subsequent creations followed the Orcs during their rebellion and escape.

HARPY

Like the Centaurs, Harpies are Beastmen. Half-human and half-bird of prey, they were originally used as scouts, messengers and skirmishers in the Wizards' armies. The Orcs adopted them as allies and see them as favored children of Father Sky. Very different characteristics have evolved in Harpies born from such diverse species as ravens, eagles, or vultures. The Harpies who settled in the Pao islands were created from various tropical raptors native to the Eastern jungles, which explains their multi-colored plumage.

WYVERN

Though Wyverns resemble small Dragons, they are in fact magical beasts, born in the Mythic Age by the "mutation" of giant lizards that were exposed to a nexus of Air magic.

They have large, bat-like wings and a dragon's head atop a supple, cat-like body covered with reptilian scales. They can ravage ranks of armies with their teeth and claws, but they are especially feared for their "Storm Breath", which combines a violent gust of wind with a sizzling lightning bolt.

Some Orc tribes have domesticated Wyverns and use them as flying mounts. A typical Wyvern Rider would not only use his mount in battle, but also some kind of ranged weapon (javelins, a bow, sometimes a small ballista or arbalest mounted on the Wyvern's saddle).

In the Pao islands, Wyverns are called "Pao Kaïs", which simply means "Blind Judges".

INFERNO BOOK
THE LORDS OF CHAOS

SUMMARY DESCRIPTION

IN A NUTSHELL

Demons are embodiments of Chaos. They believe that the only meaningful moral value is individual freedom, and they feel no need to justify their actions. A desire to commit an act self-justifies its execution. They kill because they can, or they want to.

Aka: The Demons, Hellspawns, Children of Chaos, Lords of Chaos
Associated Colours: Black and red
Country / Kingdom: Sheogh, the Prison of Fire
Capital City: Ur-Hekal, the "Gate of the Burning Heart"

HISTORY

The Demons were spawned by Urgash the All-Encircling in mockery of the other Elder races and with the sole purpose of corrupting the world that Asha had made. The Demons are scarred by Urgash's primal resentment against Asha. What has been created, they must destroy, what has been organized, they must bring Chaos to.

They live in a constant state of change, obeying their every urge. Essentially, they either exist as clay shaped by their own changing desire or as a destructive force imposing this desire. To lead them, Urgash created the six Demon Overlords, twisted counterparts to Asha's children, the Elemental Dragons.

Each Overlord was given dominion over a different aspect of Urgash's unbridled passions. The greatest Demon incursion in historical times was known as the Wars of Fire. Raging across the land, the Demons brought low the Kingdom of Angels and nearly destroyed Ashan. Only the sacrifice of Sar-Elam, the Seventh Dragon, bound them up in the Prison-world of Sheogh, banishing them from Ashan for what he thought was eternity.

However, unbeknownst to Sar-Elam, the Prison had a built-in flaw. During a lunar eclipse, when the Moon is shadowed by Ashan, the prison is weakened sufficiently for the Demons to escape. The first eclipse after the creation of the Prison produced a spectacular result. Thousands of demons rushed forth to ravage the land. Only the timely creation of the Orcs prevented the Demon hordes from overrunning the known world.

After this defeat, a civil war erupted in Sheogh. One by one, the Demon Overlords were assaulted in their fiefs. Their fortresses were cast down and their guards slaughtered, but no one claimed responsibility. Fearing each other, the Overlords went to war amongst themselves, and when the dust settled, none remained standing. A single Sovereign rose to take their place. His origins obscure, his face a mystery, he would only be referred to as Kha-Beleth... Kha-Beleth immediately set his mind on a single purpose: uniting the Demons in a relentless drive to fulfil the prophecy of the Dark

SAR-SHAZZAR'S PROPHECY

Sar-Shazzar, one of the seven disciples of Sar-Elam, had a vision that would be known as the Prophecy of the Dark Messiah, in which he foresaw the end of the prison-world of Sheogh and the ultimate triumph of the Demons.

THE PROPHECY OF THE DARK MESSIAH

Attested by My Lord Sar-Shazzar on this eleventh day of the month of the Shining Star, in the Sixty-Seventh Year of the Seventh Dragon.

Ten centuries shall the fortress stand
Walls of spirit wrapped in walls of fire
To one not yet born, man and not man
His legacy written in ashes

Eight centuries shall the raptor fly
Before the greater beast
The claw is always bloody that rends the wing
  in flight
Men who abandon a god
And strike down those who follow them
Until dragon's wrath

Six centuries the daughter of fire
Shall tarry before her time comes
Knowing not her true self
Bride and not bride
She wears many crowns not her own
And her glory is everlasting torment

Four centuries and more
Shall the dead wage war on the living
Great in spirit and in power
The Mother's milk poisoned in their mouths
Murderers who would save all
Revelation broken in their hands

Two centuries of the usurper
Hailed as rightful, hailed as righteous
The hart leaps higher than the hawk can soar
As a king, not king, looks down, an eagle
Clawed hands have laid the crown upon his head
And placed the throne before him

One century of blood and strife
The moon shall darken and none know why
Blood in the skies
Of one who was man but not man
Only son to He who stands in the fire

Last daughter of an ancient line
A sacrifice to history
The power of his ancient enemy
Exalts his blood, opens the gate
A son's loving gift to a father he knows not
Ten centuries, and that is all.

Messiah foretold in Sar-Shazzar's famous poem. He considers that Demons have a right to live freely within and without Sheogh, and he is determined to expose, if not impose, his people's right to an equal place amongst the children of the Dragon Gods.

GEOGRAPHIC LOCATION

Demons don't live on the surface of Ashan, but deep in its bowels, in the prison-realm of Sheogh, a spiritual enclosure confined in the planet's fiery core.

SOCIAL ORGANIZATION

Demons are organized into a rough hierarchy based on power, with the stronger bullying the weaker into obedience. The slightest disagreement or disobedience is met with swift and severe punishment.

Originally, the Demons were led by six Princes, legates of the six Overlords. Their own "vassals" usually styled themselves Lords of sorts and claimed some section of their particular hell as their own. The strongest Lords held cities or positions in their Prince's court, which they guarded jealously.

At the time of the Second Eclipse, the Overlords disappeared in the turmoil of the civil war within Sheogh. Demons, being a pragmatic lot, soon adjusted to having the newcomer Kha-Beleth as their sole Sovereign.

THE DEMON OVERLORDS

Created by Urgash as a gesture of defiance towards his sister Asha, the Demon Overlords represent not merely the forces of Chaos but also a reflection of Urgash's own frustrations and yearnings.

UR-HEKAL

Demon Overlord of Hate.

The weapon of Urgash's endless enmity against the universe and even his own creations, he reigns over impulsive fiery rage and cold, calculated hatred.

The most "subtle" of the Demon Overlords, he governed the largest realm on Sheogh. Sheogh's capital city is named after him.

UR-KHRAG

Demon Overlord of Destruction.

Representing the most obvious form of Chaos, he is the embodiment of one of its greatest powers: Entropy.

The Lords of Destruction generally lead the infernal legions to battle.

UR-AAZHEEL

Demon Overlord of Proliferation.

The aspect of Chaos that represents uncontrolled growth and mutation; the force of creation but without system; order or structure.

UR-VOMOCH

Demon Overlord of Voracity.

Represents the insatiable appetite of Chaos; the uncontrollable need to move, to seek, to consume. Infinite greed or wanton lust are his domains.

UR-TRAGGAL

Demon Overlord of Pain.

Tormentor and victim, a channel for the constant searing agony suffered by Urgash.

UR-JUBAAL

Demon Overlord of Madness.

Reigns over the unbalanced, infuriated and unpredictable mind that is ruled by Chaos. A visionary and a fool, a prophet and a trickster.

PHYSICAL DESCRIPTION

Demons are "alien" beings, hard to describe. Their chaotic nature makes them all unique, different within the same "species" and even from one moment to the other. However, they still share some common traits, and can be classified into general categories.

To adapt to the furnace that is Sheogh, they have grown a thick leathery hide, often covered by "organic" pieces of armour (mineral gangue, reptile scales, insect carapace). Their body shape is asymmetrical, with several excrescences (bony spikes, horns, clawed hands and feet, etc.), and one or several chaotic mutations (hooves, tentacles, barbed tail, extra pair of arms, bat-like wings, etc.). Their skin is often scarred or tattooed with intricate demonic runes that seem to be drawn with fire. It could also be covered by self-inflicted wounds suppurating with lava-like blood, or even entirely wreathed in flames.

In colour, Demon skin ranges from obsidian black to fiery red, including variations like ash grey or deep ember red.

Demonic weaponry is serrated, barbed, and spiked so as to cause maximum pain and damage, and to make any wound they inflict that much more difficult to heal.

INCUBI AND SUCCUBI

Some children of Asha, having promised themselves to Urgash and the Lords of Chaos, are reborn in Sheogh after their death as Incubi (male) or Succubi (female), creatures almost as beautiful and charismatic as Angels, but in a "carnal", sensual way.

As reincarnations of devoted Demon cultists, they have a relatively high and unusual rank in the hierarchy of Demon kind, though many of them lack the wit, devotion, or power to be anything more than servants or courtesans. Because they were not born Demons, they are not bound to Sheogh, which makes them the Demon Lords' perfect agents on Ashan.

RACIAL ABILITIES

Being unnatural beings, created in defiance of Asha's cosmic laws, the Demons are particularly vulnerable to the Magic of Order, and especially the sphere of Light.

On the other hand, their chaotic nature allows them to instinctively control the rules of entropy to a certain degree, which makes them luckier than most, or more precisely, never unlucky. Having spent centuries in the heart of Ashan's fiery core, the heat and lava is something the Demons have evolved to actually appreciate. As a result, they are totally immune to the harmful effects of Fire Magic.

The Incubi and Succubi benefit from the same abilities, and to support their roles as spies, infiltrators, and diplomats, they are granted additional "gifts" tailored to help them seduce and corrupt (powers of illusion, charm, and shape-shifting).

DIPLOMACY

EXTERNAL RELATIONS WITH OTHER FACTIONS

Historical allies: Dungeon (the Soulscar Clan has made a pact with the Lords of Sheogh), Academy (some Wizards have turned to Demon worshipping), other hidden Demon cultists among different factions.

Historical enemies: All the other factions of Ashan have always been united against the common threat posed by the Demons.

ACADEMY

Easy enough to lead astray. Dangle power in front of them and they'll sell their own mothers. When the time comes, they'll stand with us or they'll die.

DUNGEON

False faces and empty hearts. There's something going on in their underground lairs that needs to be cleansed by fire... if we can ever find it.

FORTRESS

Tough, stubborn, and steadfast. That's why they'll be broken in the end.

HAVEN

Holy fools. We've written their history in blood.

NECROPOLIS

No matter how many corpses they throw in our way, we'll burn their cold hearts to ashes. They know just enough of the truth to be dangerous.

STRONGHOLD

Our blood is in their veins. Sooner or later, they'll realize that, and take their rightful place. Until then, they make good sport to hunt.

SYLVAN

Watch the woods burn, watch the Elves run for cover, watch the Elves die.

SANCTUARY

Balance, peace, tranquility... imagine, an entire people whose goal in life is boredom. When Urgash frees us we'll see if they taste like fish or chicken.

INTERNAL DISSENSIONS

Even without the Overlords to drive them, the Demons remain split into six main groups, conditioned by the aspects of Urgash (Hate, Destruction, Pain, Madness, Voracity, Proliferation). Sheogh is constantly ravaged by conflicts rising between these groups, or between rival Demon Lords. Any Demon can become a Lord, if he truly wills it, but, except for Kha-Beleth, no leader lasts long in Sheogh.

CULTURE

CORE PHILOSOPHY

"Might makes Right" – the ability to commit an act is sufficient justification to do it. Conquer, plunder and rape the weak – or not, as you wish – indulge yourself in selfish pleasures, convert the fools who do not understand the true meaning of "liberty". Power is to be taken by the strong and lorded over the weak.

RELIGION

Demons don't really worship their progenitor, Urgash. Which is to be expected, considering that the conscience of the Primordial Dragon of Chaos is too absorbed by its own ravings to pay much attention to his children.

MAGIC

Demon magic is drawn from raw Chaos and destructive by nature. In its simplest form, it manifests as blasts of pure destruction. Overall, Demons show an unsurpassed ability to use corrupted versions of the "regular" elemental manifestations of Magic, with an unsurprising predilection for the sphere of Fire, and a no less expected rejection of the sphere of Light.

SYMBOLS

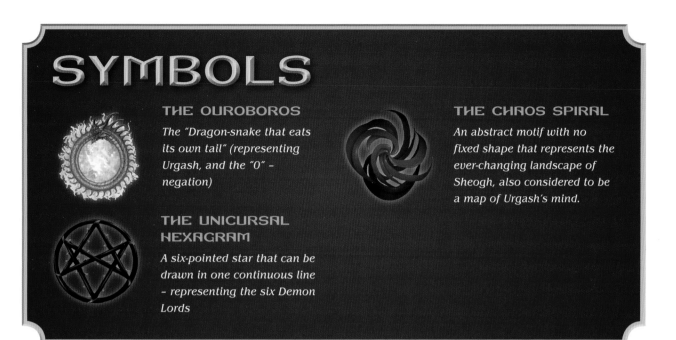

THE OUROBOROS

The "Dragon-snake that eats its own tail" (representing Urgash, and the "0" – negation)

THE UNICURSAL HEXAGRAM

A six-pointed star that can be drawn in one continuous line – representing the six Demon Lords

THE CHAOS SPIRAL

An abstract motif with no fixed shape that represents the ever-changing landscape of Sheogh, also considered to be a map of Urgash's mind.

ARCHITECTURE

Demon architecture is built entirely by slave labour and designed to intimidate. Primary materials are blocks of basalt, red-hot metal, and semi-solid lava, sculpted by Chaos magic. There's no basic shape for a given building but they are always massive and organic, with curved angles covered by serrated excrescences and spikes. Walls are thick and high. Demonic heads, gaping mouths and lurking eyes often protrude from their surface. Some of these organic elements feel as if they were "alive". The buildings often float dozens of feet above the ground, perched on jagged rock formations. This makes the whole construction suitably threatening, but also eminently impractical.

WARFARE

ON THE BATTLEFIELD

The entire nation of Demons is an army. Each one lives only to ravage and destroy, and is quite capable of wreaking tremendous havoc on his own. Forged together into a disciplined army, they would be nearly unstoppable. Fortunately for their enemies, instilling that discipline is harder than it looks, and the lesser demons often need to be driven along by massive, whip-wielding taskmasters.

If the mere intimidating presence of the Demon legions on the battlefield isn't enough, they'll use every trick at their disposal – mind control, shape-shifting, fear spells, etc. Ranged attacks and attacks from above come next. Only then, once the enemy has been sufficiently softened up, will the demonic forces charge. If they hold enough discipline, they generally power straight through anything opposing them. If not, they turn into a ravenous mob.

Demons also have a wicked ace up their sleeves: their "Gating" ability allows them to summon instant reinforcements from their prison-realm, or to teleport on the field of battle.

ICONIC INFERNO HERO

THE HERETIC

The Heretics are not "true" Demons but Humans (or Elves, Dwarves...) who have thrown aside their loyalty to their true Dragon Gods and embraced the cause of Chaos. This status is reserved for the Demon-worshippers who served their masters well and who are not already great masters of Chaos magic.

"Blessed" by Urgash for their conversion, they endure an excruciating ritual that will corrupt their flesh and soul, but also confer upon them the power to channel the fires of Sheogh and command its minions. Their corrupted body is now hidden in a semi-sentient armour they cannot remove, and they will often be seen at the front line of the Demon legions, as they lead them to ravage the surface of Ashan.

ICONIC INFERNO TROOPS

CERBERUS

Hell Hounds, or Cerberii, are servants of Ur-Vomoch, the Demon Overlord of Voracity. These multi-headed, fire breathing mastiffs outclass even the saber-toothed tigers or dire wolves in size, speed and ferocity. Their powerful and extensible maw is superbly adapted for clutching their prey and swallowing it whole, whatever their size.

JUGGERNAUT

Servants of Ur-Khrag, the Demon Overlord of Destruction, Juggernauts are easily identified by their immense horns and their basalt-covered fists and hooves. In battle, they rush violently (and sometimes blindly) into enemy lines, impaling their foes with their horns, crushing them with a swing of their massive arms, or trampling them to a bloody pulp. When needed, they even make good battering rams.

PIT FIEND

Defeated, wounded and jailed, Urgash, the Primordial Dragon of Chaos, is consumed by hatred for his sister Asha and her Creation. Ur-Hekal, Demon Overlord of Hate, is the expression of that endless enmity, and the mighty Pit Fiends are his most spectacular agents. It is said that the only creature a Pit Fiend does not hate is itself, and even that is open for discussion.

SYLVAN BOOK
THE ELF CLANS

SUMMARY DESCRIPTION

IN A NUTSHELL

The Elves are graceful and patient souls who live in close harmony with the lands and forests. They are in tune with Sylanna, the Dragon of Earth. Its deliberate nature and ancient wisdom are reflected in their approach to life and worship. Druids, warriors and hunters, particularly gifted in Nature Magic, they are friendly with the magical beasts of the Wild (Direwolves, Unicorns, Griffins...), and the Nature Spirits, or "Faeries" (Dryads, Sprites, Pixies, Treants...). Distrustful of cities, they keep to their ancient ways, view the forests and living things as their responsibilities, and do not shrink from punishing those who defile them.

Aka: The Wood Elves

Associated Colours: Green, brown and silver.

Country / Kingdom: Irollan, the forest maze

Capital City: There are four capitals, changing each season: Syris Thalla, Syris Vaniel, Syris Lothran and Syris Wynna.

HISTORY

During the first Eclipse and the war of the Blood Moon, the Elves were the first target of the Demon legions. It was they who first summoned forth the other nations to do battle against the children of Chaos, and many of the great generals of that war were Elves. Great swaths of the Elf forests were burned away by the Demons, scarring the land and poisoning the waters. Once the fighting was over, the Elves retreated to their wounded kingdom and spent almost two centuries restoring it, planting new groves, cleansing the waters, and expelling the slightest bit of Demon taint from their lands.

A few years before the Second Eclipse, his head turned by a band of flatterers, High King Arniel decided that Elf power was too decentralized, and that the traditional way of electing the supreme ruler (through a vision shared by the Druids) was unreliable. His solution was to usurp the powers of the local Elf kings, strip the Druids of their authority, and make his own title hereditary. Among the various rebels that clashed with him, the most tragically famous is Queen Tuidhana. She declared her kingdom, located at the north-western border of the Holy Empire, independent from the High King. The greedy knights of the Holy Emperor, Liam Falcon, seized the occasion to invade Tuidhana's lands, and Arniel did not lift a finger to help her. Desperate to protect her people, Tuidhana turned to the few surviving Faceless. They were willing to help her for a price. In exchange for their help her people were to convert to Malassa, the Dragon Goddess of Darkness. The Dark Elves were born.

The conflict between Arniel and Tuidhana escalated into open war, until Brythigga, the Mother of Trees and home of the original royal dwelling, was burned to the ground, leaving a blackened scar on the earth where nothing would ever grow again.

High King Arniel was caught inside the conflagration and burned alive. The Dark Elves were accused. In a gesture of mercy, Vaniel, Arniel's successor, offered Tuidhana's people safe passage out of Irollan. They could never return, but for one week, he would hold back the forces howling for vengeance. After that time, he would personally lead his armies to wipe out all the remaining rebels. Most of the Dark Elves chose to leave and the Faceless led them underground, on the Dwarf border. A few decided to stay on their native land; they were all slain by Vaniel's soldiers.

The place where Brythigga had stood was stricken from the maps, and to this day no Elf will go there. Another Mother of Trees has been consecrated, hidden deep within the forests, but no Elf will speak of her to outsiders. Vaniel eventually discovered that Demons were involved in the burning of Brythigga. He decided to apologize to the Dark Elves and offer them amnesty. They refused unanimously.

Centuries passed, and tensions remained high between the Elves and their changed brethren. Vaniel died in 756, and was succeeded by Alaron. The new King's eye turned away from the forest, and slowly he re-established stronger ties with the other nations.

He provided aid to the Wizards of the Silver Cities in their wars against the Necromancers, and encouraged traders to come to the Elf borders. He also led the Elf armies out of the forest for the ill-fated Gray Alliance, which defeated the Demon incursion of the Fifth Eclipse.

GEOGRAPHIC LOCATION

There are four major cities within the Elven realm, each serving as a seasonal capital for the king and his court. The capital changes at the solstices and equinoxes, and each city subtly tries to outdo the others. Syris Thalla (New Green) is the spring capital, located in the west. Syris Vaniel (Golden Sun) is the southern and summer capital. Syris Lothran (Blood Leaf) is the fall capital, and is located in the east, close to the Holy Empire border. Syris Wynna (White Wind) is the northern capital, and it rules in winter. The changing of the capital is a major event in the Elf calendar, and the procession of the royal court from city to city is a magnificent sight to behold.

SOCIAL ORGANIZATION

There is a High King of the Elves, and there are many other kings and queens below him. The High King rules from the central court, and once he is chosen his word is law. The process of choosing a king falls to the Druids, who fast and endure the sweatlodge until they have a common vision of who the new ruler should be. The decision has to be unanimous, and the Druids will stay in the sweat lodge without sustenance for as longas it takes.

There are several castes in the Elf society, but the more important ones are the Hunters, the Blade Dancers and the Druids.

PHYSICAL DESCRIPTION

Elven physiology is remarkably similar to that of Humans. The main visible differences are the Elves' pointed ears (designed to funnel sounds) and their wide slanted eyes (well adapted to seeing in low-light). A typical Elf is a bit taller than a Human, but very lean. Elves have no body hair, save that on their heads, and males cannot grow beards or mustaches.

Most Elves have a very pale skin. Hair and eye colour varies widely. According to the Human aesthetic canons, the Elves' features are delicate, their motions graceful, their voice soft and their language melodious. Elves dress for the woods, which is to say light clothing in summer and spring, heavier fabrics in fall and winter and earth tones in either case. Leather and fur are favoured, as are personal decorations made of natural items – flowers, amber, precious stones, shells, or polished pieces of exotic wood. Elves don't go in much for metal jewellery or armour, except if they are made of Starsilver, the lightweight but incredibly hard metal that fell from the sky in the mythic Age.

Elves are also fond of tattooing, writing their life's long story on their skin. The older the Elf, the more of his body is likely to be adorned with the record of his days. Youngsters who fill their skin with designs before the first hundred years have passed are laughed at - they'll no doubt need the space later.

RACIAL ABILITIES

Elves have a lifespan measured in centuries, but they never seem to age past their "maturity". In addition to their longevity, the Elves are blessed with heightened vision and hearing and exceptional agility.

DIPLOMACY

EXTERNAL RELATIONS WITH OTHER FACTIONS

Historical allies: Haven, Fortress, and, to a lesser extent, Academy– they all formed an alliance in the past against the Demons.

Historical enemies: Dungeon (their enemy brothers, with whom they share a bitter history), Inferno, Necropolis (they espouse a philosophy diametrically opposed to the Elves).

DUNGEON

Our shadowy brethren, the dark reflection in our mirror. It is better that such things be banished from our realms. Let them feed upon each other in the Darkness, and foul our air no longer.

FORTRESS

The little beard-brothers, so fierce and determined on the outside, so fearful on the inside. They think they dig deep, but the Earth barely notices the scratches they make on her skin.

NECROPOLIS

We viewed them as foolish... life is fleeting and precious, yet they cannot wait to end it. But they came to suck our forests dry and we understood our mistake. We pushed them back to their barren wasteland, and they will not cross our borders again.

ACADEMY

Dabblers who seek to take the cosmos and put it in tiny boxes. They seek after knowledge but search blindly, preferring to see a single leaf rather than the whole forest.

HAVEN

Brave and determined and oh-so-brief, these children flicker past like mayflies. Everything is now and hurry and we cannot relate to them, for they hear the sands in the hourglass falling down, down, down.

INFERNO

Abomination and foulness, they have no place here, and the very earth cries out beneath their feet. They are a contagion that must be cleansed.

STRONGHOLD

How odd is it that the unnatural ones are so close to nature? We could understand each other better, I think.

SANCTUARY

Water and Earth are both essential to life and nourishment. Although we live far apart and rarely meet, the ways of the Nagas are much like ours. We see in them the stewards of the waters as we are the stewards of the forests.

INTERNAL DISSENSIONS

The Sea Elves are different from their Irollan cousins. A long time ago these Elves belonged to the Shantiri Empire, but now they are gypsies of the ocean, wandering the seas of Ashan on makeshift vessels created with trees sung into the shapes of boats. They worship both Sylanna (for her gifts) and Shalassa (for her hospitality). Each Sea Elf belongs to a certain clan, called the crew, to which he remains fiercely loyal.

CULTURE

CORE PHILOSOPHY

"Live and let live… within the Harmony". Feel the living world all around you. All things are a part of it, both the foulest and the fairest. Together we are the threads that make up the fabric of existence.

RELIGION

The majority of Elves still seek protection from the Dragon of Earth. They in turn have become guardians of the Earth and especially all of the life, whether plant or animal, that grows from it.

MAGIC

The Earth governs the harmony of Nature including the mineral, plant and animal realms. It is related to stone, wood and flesh. It also represents instinct and the awareness in the world. The Elves call upon Earth magic to protect Asha's initial creation, her garden, venerating the first tree. Magic comes naturally to them, for they know it is theirs when their purpose is clear. They are guardians of life itself.

ARCHITECTURE

Elven cities are more in the air than on the ground. The Elves long ago mastered the art of convincing trees to grow to their desires, and as such they have created great canopies above the forest floor upon which they build their cities. Ladders, rope bridges, and other such devices connect the various levels of these treeborne cities. Kings and nobles dwell on the higher levels, while the common folk live closer to the ground.

Elven cities do have a ground component. The Elves rely on the trees to guard their cities better than any wall ever could.

SYMBOLS

BRYTHIGGA

The image of the World Tree, Brythigga, is the most potent Elf symbol. A tree's roots lie deep in the ground. They are connected with traditions, wisdom, the forgotten lore and buried secrets of the Underworld. A tree's trunk stands still and solid. It is connected with courage, protection, and the regenerative powers of Nature. A tree's branches reach for the stars. They are connected with the dreams and visions, the imaginative power, and the constant will to spiritual awakening. A tree's foliage is connected to seasonal changes, the cycle of life and death.

Together, all these elements reflect the guiding values of Elf society, and the best possible illustration of their concept of "Harmony".

THE TRIPLE KNOT

The triple knot is a simpler, more common symbol of the Harmony. It refers to various important triads: the three reigns of Nature – mineral, plant and animal; the cycle of life, death and rebirth as represented in Nature – seed, flower and fruit; and also the three castes in the Elf society: Hunters, Blade Dancer and Druids. The crossing lines show that these aspects are always interconnected.

WARFARE

ON THE BATTLEFIELD

Lightly armoured and swift of foot, Elf warriors are designed for speed and striking power. Bows and slings are standard issue, as are short curved swords, javelins and throwing knives. Shields are rarely used, with the occasional exception of small wooden bucklers.

Leather armour of all varieties is about as heavy as it usually gets, though nobles and commanders sometimes wear Starsilver. Elven cavalry is mostly light cavalry, again designed for speed and maneuverability over shock power. Only the elite Unicorn Riders – the closest the Elves come to the knights of the Holy Empire - will use large shields and lances to drive their point home.

Elf armies are also composed of a fluid array of allied spirit units. Pixies and Sprites from the Fairy Folk, Treants and Dryads from the deep forest, Unicorns from sacred groves, all join the Elves willingly in their battles. Tied to the Elves and beholden to Sylanna, they instinctively appear when and where they are needed.

Unsurprisingly, Elves hate a stand-up fight and prefer guerilla tactics. To an Elf general, the perfect battle is one in which the enemy never sees a single Elf. Maneuverability is the key to Elf tactics – they are past masters of retreating to draw the enemy into an advantageous position for them. Land means nothing to them – in a fight they concentrate on picking an enemy army apart.

Usually they will screen their main force with a line of skirmishers who will serve to draw opponents into traps, where they can be pounded with arrows from three sides. The archers and Druids will fire from cover, move on, and fire again. The more confusion they can sow with arrow fire and long range spells, the better.

ICONIC SYLVAN HERO

THE RANGER

The Rangers are the Wardens of Irollan, Sylanna's chosen warriors. They are expert with the bow and the sword, wise in the ways of the forest, and able to commune with the beasts of the wild and the spirits of Nature.

When an Elf child is chosen to follow the path of the Ranger, he receives advanced training from the three main castes of Elf society:

- The Hunters teach him how to use the bow, the spear, the javelin and the knife, how to forage for food, how to find his way and track prey, how to be stealthy, how to tame and train the wild beasts.
- The Blade Dancers initiate him to their martial techniques; barehand fighting, acrobatics, evasion, and the way of the twin swords.
- Finally, the Druids share with him their knowledge of the Spirit Lore and of Earth Magic. When the child is deemed ready, he is sent into the deep forest, to find his totem spirit. When he comes back from this vision quest he has the power to shape-change into his totem, and his tribe recognizes him as a true Ranger.

ICONIC SYLVAN TROOPS

DRYAD

Upon dying, an Elf can request to be entombed inside the living trunk of a Treant. It goes without saying that close ties must exist between the Elf and his chosen vessel to make this unusual funeral ceremony possible. The living heart of the tree cradles the Elf's remains, curled in a foetal position. The trunk of the Treant forms a matrix and its sap embalm the body, transforming it over a period of months. The evolution is similar to a cocoon; length and effect depend somewhat on the type of Treant, the Elf, the glade, and other factors.

The spirit of the Elf escapes from the cycle of reincarnation, returning to Ashan as a forest spirit known as a Dryad. Dryads take on the image of the Treant that gave them birth. They are attached body and spirit to their progenitors. Both creatures will protect and support each other until their deaths. Dryads can sing trees into shape to create tools, weapons and even buildings for their Elven relatives.

A chorus of Dryads can form an ancient tree into the foundations of an Elven city. In exceedingly rare and exceptional cases, their combined harmonics can even induce the ponderous march of the forest itself.

PIXIE

A Pixie is a spirit of nature born among flowers whose scent will remain with it throughout its life. The type of flower will determine the aspect, personality and powers of the Pixie. Pixies manifest as miniature, childish humanoids, no more than one foot in size. They have oddly coloured skin, hair and eyes, and they sport wings that look like a butterfly's but are in fact leaves or petals from their associated flower. These wings allow them to fly with great velocity and skill. Pixies are closely tied to the turning of the seasons; they are rare in winter and relatively numerous in spring and summer.

It is important to distinguish between Pixies born from wildflowers and those from gardens. The former are rough and solitary and tend to die quickly if they are captured or domesticated. The latter, however, are accustomed to other species and can even become pets and "familiars", especially to the Elven Druids. Pixies born from a rose are a traditional gift between Elf lovers.

TREANT

Treants are rare and exceptional forest spirits that appear as large, walking trees. Living embodiments of the force of Nature and growth, they are the protectors and shepherds of all trees, plants and flowers. They are born only on sacred soil deep within the forests of Irollan, near a Dragon vein or nexus attuned to the essence of Earth.

They are natural allies of the Elves and share a unique, symbiotic relationship with those who choose to be buried within their trunks and be reborn as Dryads.

NECROPOLIS BOOK
THE SPIDER CULT

SUMMARY DESCRIPTION

IN A NUTSHELL

Necromancers began as a splinter sect of the Wizards, and grew into a powerful nation. They worship the "Death" aspect of Asha. Their interpretation of the Goddess's darkest aspect is fanatical, emphasizing death alone and exalting the state of unlife to which all Necromancers aspire. Necromancers study Death Magic in order to become eternal, they learn how to control the spirits of the deceased (ghosts) or how to raise the dead from their graves (skeletons, zombies).

Aka: The Necromancers, the Undead, the Death Lords
Associated Colours: Black, white and fluorescent (toxic) green
Country / Kingdom: Heresh, the Valley of Dust
Capital City: Al-Bétyl, the Dark Jewel, then Nar-Ankar, the Wailing Needle

HISTORY

As with many things that concern magic, Necromancy began as part of the legacy of Sar-Elam, the great wizard who became the Seventh Dragon. His most gifted disciple was Sar-Shazzar, who went on to carve his own place in history. Sar-Shazzar himself had a talented student, named Belketh.

In an age when the world was young and vibrant and much of magic was in doing, building, and experimenting, Belketh was a thinker and philosopher, who was fascinated with the principles and passages of death - must we all?

Do we all? Where does the soul go? What exactly ends with death, and what begins? Belketh turned less and less to the teachings of his master and more and more to his own reflections and investigations. At a critical moment he uncovered an ancient manuscript, a part of the writings of Sar-Elam collectively known as the Revelations of the Seventh Dragon. This particular chapter detailed the worship of Asha through its least understood and most feared aspect.

Belketh was struck by the conviction that this countenance of Asha was all-embracing and all-encompassing and that it could lead him on the higher path to the power of the immortal soul. Belketh called his new philosophy "Necromancy", and it proved immediately popular among his fellow Wizards in the Seven Cities. Necromantic experimentations began in Belketh's city, Al-Betyl. Soon, the first Undead servants (ghosts and animated corpses) rose from the grave and were immediately pressed into use to help suppress the revolt of the Orcs and Beastmen.

From that point on, the Necromancers grew steadily in power and influence, until such time as the rulers of the Seven Cities, fearing their ever-increasing strength and numbers, initiated a large-scale persecution,

ranging from the seizing of their properties, to banishment, to the spectacle of public executions. This brought about a long and gruesome civil war, one that the Necromancers lost. Forced to settle in the valleys of Heresh, the Necromancers declared their independence, using the city of Nar-Heresh as their base of operations to plan their revenge.

In 813 YSD, the Necromancers launched a surprise assault on the Wizard cities, now united into a new federation: the Silver League. Undead armies swarmed across the borders of Heresh, destroying everything in their path. For ten years the conflict raged and the massive waves of destructive magic used by both sides left much of the land uninhabitable. The once fertile valleys of Heresh were "vitrified" and became a barren wasteland, filled with bones and laments. The Wizards once again gained the upper hand. The Necromancers were utterly defeated, their armies scattered and their kingdom shattered. This conflict would be known as the War of the Broken Staff.

The surviving Necromancers went into hiding. It took them a couple of centuries to recoup their strength. In 973 YSD, they rose again as a strong nation under the leadership of the Death Lord Arantir, who would focus all his resources on preventing the coming of the Dark Messiah. He would eventually fail in his task and be slain by the Chosen of Chaos...

GEOGRAPHIC LOCATION

In the years 751-770 YSD, the Necromancers were persecuted, and they sought shelter in Nar-Heresh, the easternmost city of the Wizard federation. During the War of the Broken Staff (813-822 YSD), the Wizards launched a massive assault on Heresh, and much of its once fertile valley was rendered uninhabitable, foul magics bubbling up through its sands and dissolving any fool who dared venture in. The surviving Necromancers fled underground, losing themselves among the mazes of caverns and crypts.

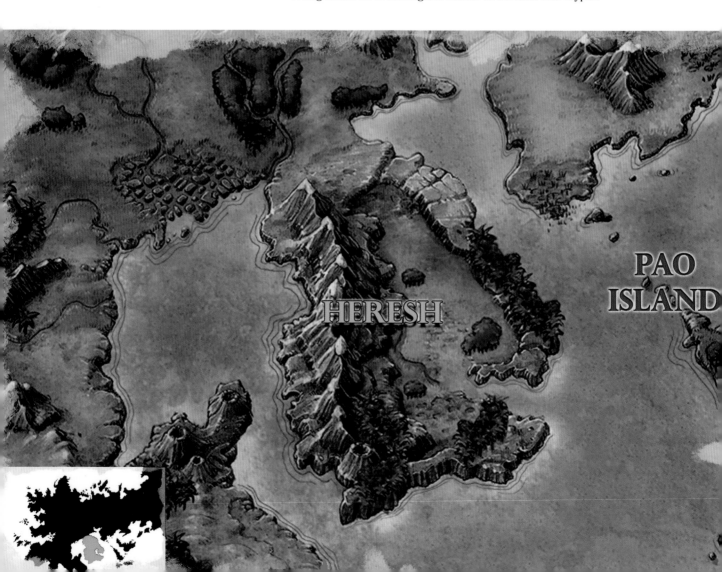

HERESH

PAO ISLAND

SOCIAL ORGANIZATION

The majority of the Necromancers are lower ranking citizens, soldiers, temple initiates and acolytes. They are supervised by the priests of the Spider Goddess and the "Death Knights" who lead the armies of Heresh on the battlefield. These higher ranking Necromancers are given a life-prolonging elixir that they must mix with their food. "Milked" from the venom of the Namtarus, the Goddess's sacred spiders, this "treatment" turns them into Asakkus, or "Liches". The "Death Lords", Necromancers and Death Knights of the highest rank are embraced by their Spider Goddess herself to die and be reborn as Akhkharus, or "Vampires". They undergo an excruciating ritual but gain a rejuvenated body, cleansed from all defects. They are "technically" immortal and even age backwards. The Elder Vampires who sit in the ruling council of Heresh all appear to be in their mid-twenties, beautiful and unchanging.

PHYSCIAL DESCRIPTION

(Only the "Human" Necromancers will be described here, although, like the Wizards, they can be of any origins - Human, Elf, Dwarf, etc.).

Heresh is a barren wasteland, baked by a scorching sun, another good reason for the Necromancers to spend most of their time in the cool darkness of their crypts and libraries. As a result, their skin is not tanned like that of their Wizard neighbours, but pale white, almost translucent. Uniformity and austerity are the rules of Necromancer fashion. They all wear simple robes (dark green, black, or white, depending on their caste and rank) and shave their hair (head, face and body). The only decorations that are allowed are symbols of the Spider Goddess (in all forms and motifs, including tattoos, piercings or brandings). Most of the Necromancers are still "mortal", and they look relatively normal, except for their pale skin and shaved bodies.

When chosen to lead their nation and turned into Liches, they absorb the venom of the Namtarus, which desiccate their bodies and frees them from the passions of the flesh. They keep aging however, until they look little more than walking mummies... The venom also colours the whole of their eyes bright green.

The Vampire Lords are perfection made flesh. Their skin is preternaturally white, like an alabaster statue, and their eyes radiate a cold green light. Many also let their hair grow again, to reinforce their unique status.

RACIAL ABILITIES

The Asakkus ("Liches") gain few abilities, apart from their extended lifetime and immunity to disease and putrefaction. The Akhkharus ("Vampires"), on the other hand, are extremely powerful beings.

They don't need to eat, drink, sleep or breathe anymore. All their organs are "petrified", and it is not blood, but the sacred spider's venom that now flows in their veins. However, they need to drink human blood on a regular basis to thin this venom down, and prevent it from dissolving their body from the inside. Vampires don't feel pain, or fear, or any kind of emotion. They gain heightened senses and supernatural strength and speed. In their eyes, they have become the embodiment of Order and perfection...

Note: Vampires in Ashan can see their reflection in mirrors, are not paralyzed by a wooden stake to the heart, are not burnt by holy water or the light of the sun, don't fear garlic or silver weapons, and can't turn into bats. However, they are vulnerable to fire, and to Light magic (which damages them and all Undead creatures instead of healing them).

DIPLOMACY

EXTERNAL RELATIONS WITH OTHER FACTIONS

Historical allies: none

Historical enemies: Academy (Necromancers were dissidents in the Seven Cities, they were first persecuted, then banned and hunted), Haven (Necromancer cults in the Holy Empire were "purged" by the Church of the Light), Sylvan (they consider that the Undead don't belong to the Harmony), Inferno (they are theologically opposed).

ACADEMY

Once we walked among them and shared our truths with them. Small minds among them were ruled by fear and cast us out. So be it - they have chosen not to join us willingly, yet sooner or later every one of them shall come to our realm.

DUNGEON

They search for profane and worldly secrets, holding to their caves and shadows. They lack the vision to understand the knowledge we possess.

FORTRESS

Leave them alone and they will leave you alone. Their devotion is touching, but their eyes do not see.

SYLVAN

We are their winter, and winter always comes.

HAVEN

Angels guide them, no doubt for the Angels own good. We will follow where their armies go and take the dead they leave behind.

INFERNO

We seek the peace of death, not the ruin of desolation. Their philosophy is Chaos, impulsiveness, conflict; ours is Order, serenity, peace. At every turn, we will oppose them.

STRONGHOLD

Forced into life, they nonetheless cling to it fiercely. Such an attachment to breathing is unhealthy.

SANCTUARY

They may praise the water as deathless and timeless, but all that lies within it must one day bow before our greater truths.

INTERNAL DISSENSIONS

Apart from infrequent power struggles between rival Death Lords, the Necromancers are firmly unified under the one will of their goddess Asha.

CULTURE

CORE PHILOSOPHY

Morbid fascination for death and fanatic devotion to the cause of Asha.

"Embrace the Void. Enlightenment can be found only after the passions of the flesh have been stripped away. Time is our ally, for all things that live will someday die..."

RELIGION

Necromancers worship Asha, the Primordial Dragon of Order, in a twisted version of her "Death" aspect.The Necromancers reject Chaos and disorder, thus they reject emotions, appetites and ultimately life itself. Their extreme quest for Order and serenity has led them to try and take control of time itself, so that death becomes the start of an existence they can abide. Only the most worthy qualify for this morbid unlife, while others become at best unquestioning servants and at worst eternally suffering pawns.

MAGIC

Necromancers, like all followers of Sar-Elam, do not revere the Dragons as Gods but rather as "Enlightened Beings" and powerful spiritual symbols. They consider that Magic lies within them and must be developed through extensive study of arcane lore (mainly the teachings of Sar-Elam) and a rigorous discipline. That said, they have a deep respect for Asha, which is almost religious in nature and another point of dissension with their (once) fellow Wizards.

Necromancers have an obvious fascination for Prime Magic, which grants them control over Time, Space, and the Spirit. Among the Elemental spheres they favour Darkness and Earth, which offer interesting combinations with their Undead minions. To interact with the spirits of the Dead, they have developed their own branch of Dark magic, which they call Necromancy.

ARCHITECTURE

Apart from the single spire of Nar-Ankar, also called the "Wailing Needle", which is a reminder of their early days in the Seven Cities when towers filled the landscape, Necromancer architecture is frighteningly uniform. The Necromancers' devotion to Order is reflected in their obsession for symmetry and sharp, angular shapes. Pyramids and obelisks are their archetypal buildings, unadorned except for the ever-present symbols of their Spider Goddess. Their favourite construction material is the cracked black stone of the plains of Heresh, making it seem as if entire cities are drinking in the light of day and swallowing it down.

SYMBOL

THE DEATH SPIDER

In his first lectures, Belketh often referred to the image of Asha as a spider, spinning the web of life, administering death through her poisonous mandibles when one's allotted time was up. The Necromancers took the Spider to symbolize death as the answer to all, the reduction of existence to its purest and most changeless form.

WARFARE

ON THE BATTLEFIELD

Necromancers, like Wizards, are rarely seen on the front lines. They usually stay in the rear echelon, either as a command cadre, or as support units. Otherwise, Undead armies consist of wave after wave of the walking dead, countless in number, infinitely obedient, immune to fear or pain. These lesser Undead are generally slow and clumsy, but they have the numbers to drown their enemies, and the ranks of the dead enemies are "raised" to replace their own fallen lines.

Necromancers also employ Ghosts in battle, for quick surgical strikes. In many ways, Ghosts are to the Death Lords what the Djinns are to the Wizards. Necromancers will generally press an attack for hours, knowing full well this is one of their advantages. Their troops, after all, never get tired.

ICONIC NECROPOLIS HERO

THE DEATH KNIGHT

The Death Knight preaches the merits of unlife and eagerly converts both the willing and the dead. Those who stand against the will of the Spider Goddess in the crusade to forcefully maintain the balance of Life and Death, must be victorious or be enlisted as a part of the congregation. Many Death Knights become obsessed with their role and come to believe that they must kill everything until Asha sends someone capable of stopping them. Asha uses all.

ICONIC NECROPOLIS TROOPS

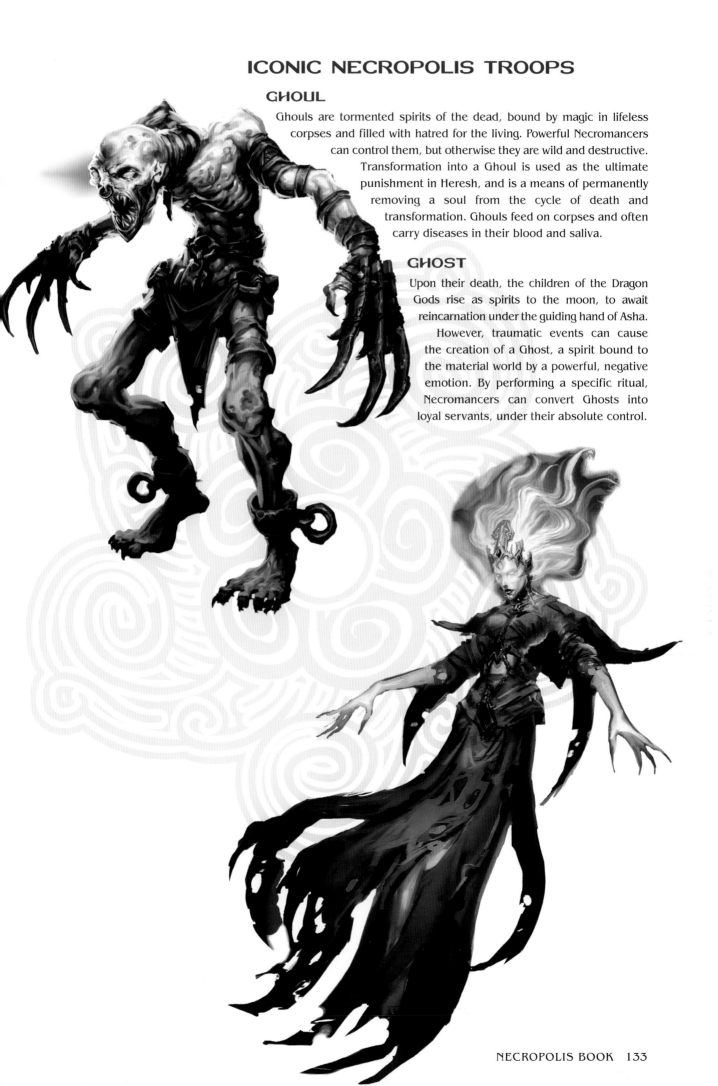

GHOUL

Ghouls are tormented spirits of the dead, bound by magic in lifeless corpses and filled with hatred for the living. Powerful Necromancers can control them, but otherwise they are wild and destructive. Transformation into a Ghoul is used as the ultimate punishment in Heresh, and is a means of permanently removing a soul from the cycle of death and transformation. Ghouls feed on corpses and often carry diseases in their blood and saliva.

GHOST

Upon their death, the children of the Dragon Gods rise as spirits to the moon, to await reincarnation under the guiding hand of Asha. However, traumatic events can cause the creation of a Ghost, a spirit bound to the material world by a powerful, negative emotion. By performing a specific ritual, Necromancers can convert Ghosts into loyal servants, under their absolute control.

NAMTARU

Namtarus, or Fate Spinners, are emanations of the Mother Namtaru, an avatar of the Spider Goddess, a truly divine reflection of the Death aspect of Asha. They can either assume the form of a spider-woman hybrid or that of a female humanoid with two legs and six arms.

Worshipped by the Necromancers, who use their venom to sustain their ranks of Liches and Vampires, Namtarus will often be present at the founding of a Necropolis, like the queen of a hive, to fortify its foundations and nurture its growth.

The Namtarus regularly counsels their devotees through whisper, rhyme, and even dream. Under their protection, the Undead comb the region for lost souls which they then recruit to swell their ranks.

FORTRESS BOOK
THE LORDS UNDER THE MOUNTAIN

SUMMARY DESCRIPTION

IN A NUTSHELL

Fierce warriors, industrious blacksmiths, and masters of Rune Magic, the Dwarves are suspicious of outsiders. Wardens of the Demons (for they live closest to the "lava core" where Asha imprisoned Urgash), rivals of the Dark Elves (they compete for underground territory).

Aka: The Dwarves

Associated Colours: Fiery red and steel gray

Country / Kingdom: Grimheim, the Kingdom Under the Mountain, also known as the "Stone Halls".

Capital City: Tor Myrdal, the Fire-rumbling Fortress.

BART BRIMSTONE THE DWARF PIRATE

In a society as secluded and organized as the Dwarves', renegades are rare but not unheard of. One of them is Hilbart "Brimstone" of the Stronghammer clan, better known as Bart Brimstone, the Dwarf Pirate. Born in a clan of artisans and engineers, Brimstone was fascinated by water and believed there was great power to be harnessed in the marriage of fire and its opposite element. His research was regarded as heresy by the other Dwarves, which eventually led to Brimstone's exile. To further his knowledge of the Water element, he eventually joined a crew of Sea Elves in their travels, and ended up falling in love with the ocean and its endless possibilities. He became a pirate to fund his experiments, sailing for a time as boatswain to the infamous Crag Hack, before becoming a captain of his own. Brimstone built a fortress on a volcanic island of the Savage Sea, where he created his masterpiece: the first (and so far, only) steam-powered vehicle of Ashan, a great ship he called the Fiery Heart. Brimstone's Fiery Heart can often be found adventuring alongside Crag Hack's Revenge on the Savage Sea, anchored in Foster's Reach or engaged in battle against his archenemy, the Naga pirate hunter Uminori.

FIERY SOULS

When a Dwarf experiences a very strong emotion, for example passion, love or anger, he expresses the power of Arkath. His hair and beard go up in flames. These manifestations vary according to the Dwarf's clan. The beard of a Grimsteel Dwarf becomes a mudslide of lava, the hair of a Deepflame Dwarf a cloud of sparks...

HISTORY

The Dwarves have coalesced from a series of scattered clans into a mighty nation, capable of defending itself against all enemies. Children of the Dragon of Fire, they worship him in the deep places of the world where magma provides the only light, and in return they are taught the secrets of the forge and the hearth. The Dwarves have lengthy sagas, eddas, and histories concerning their deeds, wars, and adventures, but these are not shared with the outside world. The things they have seen and the battles they have fought within their own domain remain mysterious to the surface dwellers.

What is known of their history is that in the Ancient Age, they were part of the Shantiri Empire and influential in the forging and enchanting of their legendary weapons and Constructs. During the Wars of Fire, the Dwarf warbands joined with the other nations of Ashan to resist the Demons. But once the fighting was over, they returned to their homes under the mountains and had little to do with the other races for centuries. Tunnels were dug between the various Dwarf cities, connecting them into a honeycomb deep beneath the earth, year after year, decade after decade.

All that changed a few years before the Second Eclipse, when the first Dark Elves settled on the Dwarves' borders. A steadily deteriorating situation turned into the War Under the Mountain, in which the Dwarves, led by Hathor Deepstrider Orlandsson, crushed the Dark Elves and drove them out.

Today, the Dwarves still keep up a watchful vigilance. They observe their borders, and no one moves on their lands unseen. They befriend a precious few and expand their kingdom carefully.

GEOGRAPHIC LOCATION

The capital city of the Dwarves is Tor Myrdal, built beneath two massive volcanoes. Tradition demands that all Dwarf kings climb the mile-long

GRIMHEIM

IROLLAN

knife-edged ridge that connects their summits. Tor Myrdal is so massive and complex that no one, not even the Dwarves, know all of its passages and tunnels. Indeed, some Dwarves have a superstitious fear that someone else – not of their kin – has been adding to and modifying the tunnels for centuries, for some nefarious purpose that is as yet unknown.

The second most famous and most populous Dwarf city is Tor Hallr, known to non-Dwarves as "Beardsgate" and to the Dwarves, colloquially, as "Talltown". It is the gateway to Grimheim and the only Dwarf trading post with "the outsiders". Other major Dwarf cities include Tor Vettfang, Tor Eldrheim, Tor Hlifa, and Tor Lindhath.

SOCIAL ORGANIZATION

Dwarves define themselves by their kinship to one of the six clans, each born from a mythic ancestor, and having its own name, battle history, customs and so forth.

Clan Deepflame – Keepers of the lore and Rune-Priests of Arkath, the Dragon of Fire

Clan Grimsteel – Warriors

Clan Winterwind – Explorers and Beastmasters

Clan Stronghammer – Craftsmen and Metal-Workers

Clan Stonefist – Architects and Stone-Workers

Clan Hearthguard – Chancellors and Administrators

Although the clans have spread throughout the Dwarf kingdom and settled in all the major cities, ultimately, Dwarves always fall back on their clans. Each Dwarf city has its own king, with a council of advisors from the wealthiest and most industrious families. The King Under the Mountains is the chosen of kings among the Dwarves, and it is he who sets policy and summons them to war. Kingship is not hereditary, though it is a lifetime post.

PHYSICAL DESCRIPTION

Dwarves are short and stocky. They rarely stand much over 4 feet tall. Adult male Dwarves always wear full beards. Their hair can be any colour, but blonde is the most common. Red hair is rare and considered a good omen as it evokes the colour of their patron Dragon.

Females never grow beards or moustaches. Hairstyle is much codified and varies from clan to clan. Most Dwarves have black eyes, save for a few whose eyes are flecked with gold. These Dwarf children are systematically taken for the priesthood of Arkath.

Dwarves dress practically. They like layers of leather garb when they go journeying in the world, supplemented by plate mail and finely crafted helmets when in war. All Dwarves are armed at all times – even if it's just with a boot dagger, and a Dwarf would sooner be naked than unarmed.

RACIAL ABILITIES

As children of Arkath, Dwarves are very resistant to fire. They can grab hot coals with their bare hands without feeling any pain or having their skin burned. Also, their body temperature is so hot that they don't feel the cold's bite and don't suffer much from ice magic. Dwarves also have an innate sense of direction and depth that helps them find their way in their underground mazes.

DIPLOMACY

EXTERNAL RELATIONS WITH OTHER FACTIONS

Historical allies: Haven (the Knights), Sylvan (the Wood Elves)

Historical enemies: Inferno (the Demons), Dungeon (the Dark Elves)

SYLVAN

They are a brave lot, living in such fragile forests, that a gentle wind and a simple spark could burn to the ground in the beating of a mountain's heart.

HAVEN

A confusion. They're alternately proud and boastful, brave and cowardly, and noble and base. They'll deal fairly more than half the time, but you can never tell which half.

INFERNO

They bring fire with them, but they don't understand it. You see one, you send it back where it came from, you understand?

STRONGHOLD

Brave, honourable brutes. Think of what they could do if they had some good equipment.

SANCTUARY

Meditation is a poor substitute for craft. The fires of Arkath could steam away their cities; then they'd be as helpless as a fish out of water.

ACADEMY

The Wizards want it all and they want it now. You'd think the Dragons created the rest of us just to serve them, to hear them talk on it.

DUNGEON

There are things below ground that would freeze the balls off the bravest knight. We watch for them, and when they crawl up out of the dark, we kill them.

NECROPOLIS

They've walked in the dark places. We want nothing to do with them, and they with us, and we both like it that way.

CULTURE

CORE PHILOSOPHY

"Never yield and never lose face". Be proud of who you are. Defend your kinsmen, your homeland and your honour. Always protect the hearth.

RELIGION

The Dwarves worship Arkath, the Dragon of Fire. They and fire are old friends, and their communion is an intensely personal ritual that most outsiders have never seen. Coal and a good set of bellows are key elements of any Dwarf religious site. Ritual branding is done as part of their rites of passage, to emphasize the Dwarf belief that the soul is forged just like a pure ingot.

MAGIC

Dwarves mainly rely on Fire magic, the "ruthless" magic that consumes the weak but gives strength and purpose to the strong. Apart from the deadly fire spells, their magic is mainly used to instill strength in warriors, forge objects and help during sieges.

Runic inscriptions are omnipresent in Dwarf society and many Dwarves have runic tattoos on their skin. Each rune corresponds to a spell, an open door for communication between the physical world and the spiritual world. Runes allow the physical properties of an object to be channeled to the Rune bearer. Runes allow the physical properties of an object to be channeled to the rune bearer.

ARCHITECTURE

Dwarf warrens are built in concentric rings around a central great hall. Main avenues run off in the cardinal directions, with smaller tunnels in between. Dwarf architecture also runs in three dimensions, with plenty of stairs, wells, and galleries honeycombing the mountains under which they live.

In design, Dwarves are not fond of representational art, preferring instead geometric patterns. Their buildings, roads, and stairs are mostly built to be sturdy rather than pleasing to the eye. One decorative field the Dwarves do specialize in, however, is lava gardening. Most Dwarf families own centuries-old gardens of molten rock and carefully tended obsidian, cooled to precise specifications over the years.

The Dwarves are also skilled glassblowers, and are renowned all over Ashan for their mastery of the art of stained glass, which they usually use to decorate the inside of their houses, especially around their hearths. These great frescoes usually describe the heroic adventures of their ancestors. With the fire burning at the centre of the house, it's like the whole history of the family comes alive on the walls.

Contrary to the popular belief found in the Holy Empire, Dwarves are not obsessed by gold, a metal they use to trade with the other peoples of Ashan but deem too fragile to be useful. Instead, the social rank and wealth of a Dwarf is often demonstrated by the complexity of the glass windows and sculptures he possesses.

SYMBOLS

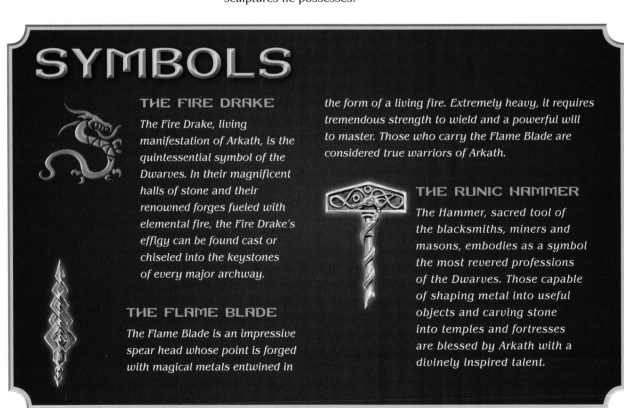

THE FIRE DRAKE

The Fire Drake, living manifestation of Arkath, is the quintessential symbol of the Dwarves. In their magnificent halls of stone and their renowned forges fueled with elemental fire, the Fire Drake's effigy can be found cast or chiseled into the keystones of every major archway.

THE FLAME BLADE

The Flame Blade is an impressive spear head whose point is forged with magical metals entwined in the form of a living fire. Extremely heavy, it requires tremendous strength to wield and a powerful will to master. Those who carry the Flame Blade are considered true warriors of Arkath.

THE RUNIC HAMMER

The Hammer, sacred tool of the blacksmiths, miners and masons, embodies as a symbol the most revered professions of the Dwarves. Those capable of shaping metal into useful objects and carving stone into temples and fortresses are blessed by Arkath with a divinely inspired talent.

WARFARE

ON THE BATTLEFIELD

The Dwarven warbands are one of the most feared fighting forces in the world. Featuring unparalleled ferocity and iron discipline, they can be mustered at a moment's notice. In combat, warbands from various cities try to outdo each other in terms of enemies killed, banners taken and the like – war is a game, and this is a way of keeping score.

The Dwarf warriors, while ferocious, are possessed of an uncanny discipline. They have been known to hold position under withering arrow fire for hours, waiting for the right moment to charge. Dwarves never, ever surrender. They fight to the death, even when the odds are hopelessly against them. The best death a Dwarf can wish for is one in battle, against impossible odds, with a witness who will someday make a song of their deeds.

While they prefer fighting underground, Dwarves do occasionally muster on the surface. In the tunnels, where large bands are less useful, they build complicated defensive fortifications and traps. Dwarves who explore unknown tunnels are called Delvers, and they are often the first line of defense against an incursion by Dark Elves, demons and the like.

Most Dwarves go into battle armed with a kite shield, a heavy single-bladed axe and a brace of daggers. They also have other weapons hidden about their person, just in case. A Dwarf is never unprepared in battle. Crossbows and siege engines are Dwarf specialties, and are vastly preferred to less complicated devices like bows, slings and the like. Dwarf ballista crews are deadly accurate, and can reload and fire fast enough to break up almost any enemy advance. Dwarves particularly excel at sieges, with their engineers and sappers working relentlessly to undermine any fortifications they face. By the same token, they excel at defensive warfare, and can turn all but the most barren position into a fortress with astonishing speed.

ICONIC FORTRESS HERO

THE RUNE PRIEST

The Rune Priest is a master of Rune Magic, which creates links with the Spirit World. By tracing symbols in stone or fire, the Rune Priests can communicate with the spiritual reflection of the elements. For instance, by talking with the stone, they can facilitate the opening of new tunnels.

The Rune Priests also preside over the rituals to honour their Dragon-God. When a Dwarf dies, they bring his body to the volcano to ensure his soul will become one with the flames.

ICONIC FORTRESS ALLIES

VALKYRIE

Valkyries are fire spirits, manifestations of Arkath. Their ashen body sports majestic wings of fire. Valkyries are born on the battlefield. When numerous Dwarves die in battle, their souls gather and, with Arkath's blessing, they spark this powerful warrior spirit into life.

BATTLE BEAR

When they travel outside of their subterranean realm, the Dwarves of the Winterwind clan often make a detour in the nearby forests to hunt and capture wild animals. That's how they gather the great bears who are then trained to fight alongside them.

FIRE GIANT

For the Dwarves, each new volcanic eruption is an important event, an opportunity to pay tribute to their Dragon-God Arkath. Many warriors volunteer to participate in a sacrificial ritual. Rune priests draw powerful symbols on their bare skin, to bind them with the sacred Fire. The volunteers then climb to the mouth of the volcano at the moment of the blast.

The few Dwarves who survive the ordeal are fused with the elements of fire and stone. They are transformed into Fire Giants, colossal beings of basalt crackling with lava. When they return to their home cities, they are revered as heroes and the chosen of Arkath.

DUNGEON BOOK
THE SHDOW-MARKED

SUMMARY DESCRIPTION

IN A NUTSHELL

The Dark Elves are underground-dwelling renegades from the Elf forests who have made a pact with the mysterious Faceless. Deadly schemers in the darkness, their whole nation is imprinted by Malassa's mark and forced to hear the constant whispers of the world.

Aka: The Dark Elves
Associated Colours: Black and purple
Country / Kingdom: Ygg-Chall, the Dark Below
Capital City: Konos, the Maze of Shadows

HISTORY

The Dark Elves were born a few years before the Second Eclipse, from the betrayal of a small nation of Elves by their monarch. During his reign, the High King Arniel decided to usurp the powers of the local Elf kings and make his own title hereditary. Queen Tuidhana refused to bow to these outrageous demands, and declared her kingdom, located at the north-western border of the Holy Empire, independent from the High King.

The greedy knights of the Holy Emperor Liam Falcon, seized the occasion to invade Tuidhana's lands. Battered by the imperial armies, Tuidhana appealed to Irollan for help, but Arniel chose to let her land suffer and her people die. Desperate to protect her people, Tuidhana turned to the few surviving Faceless. They were willing to help her for a price. In exchange for their help her people were to convert to Malassa, the Dragon Goddess of Darkness. Tuidhana accepted their offer, and the Dark Elves were born.

With the newfound powers granted by her Faceless allies, Tuidhana reaffirmed her independence. Her kingdom's freedom was recognized – at swordpoint – by Elves and Humans. An uneasy peace settled between the Elves and the Dark Elves. Twenty years passed in a rough truce, until a terrible accident sent things from bad to worse... A criminal fire was set to Brythigga, the Mother of Trees, home of the royal dwelling. The sacred tree was burned to the ground, leaving a blackened scar on the earth where nothing would ever grow again. Arniel was caught inside the conflagration and burned alive. The Dark Elves were blamed for the heinous crime.

In a gesture of mercy, Vaniel, Arniel's successor, offered Tuidhana's people safe passage out of Irollan. They could never return, but for one week, he would hold back the forces howling for vengeance. After that time, he would personally lead his armies to wipe out all the remaining rebels. Most of the Dark Elves chose to leave, and the Faceless led them underground, on the Dwarf border.

Tuidhana remained behind with only a handful of loyal followers to stand against the Elf armies massed on her border. She died a queen and a martyr, defending her lands. Vaniel eventually discovered that Demons were involved in the burning of Brythigga. He decided to apologize to the Dark Elves and offer them amnesty. They refused unanimously.

Meanwhile, the relations between Dwarves and Dark Elves, that already started tense, got worse. Both races sought many of the same resources in the dark deeps. Very soon, local skirmishes grew into an open conflict. The so-called War Under the Mountains was brutal, completely devoid of mercy as massive armies clashed in the dark. Eventually, the Dwarves crushed the Dark Elves and drove them out. Once again guided by their Faceless allies, the Dark Elves moved south, eventually settling on the ruins of the ancient Faceless kingdom of Ygg-Chall.

Since that day, the Dark Elves have prospered in their tunnels. They have grown strong and numerous, and their traders range far and wide offering irresistible deals that somehow manage to work mainly to the Dark Elves' benefit. They have made no move against either the Elves or Dwarves, nor have they tried to reconquer their old lands. Instead, they consolidate their power, and they wait.

IROLLAN

YGG CHALL

HOLY FAI
EMPIR

GEOGRAPHIC LOCATION

In its own way, the entire Dark Elf kingdom is one massive city: Konos, the maze. That being said, there are denser clutches of population here and there, each of which views itself as its own city. Major ones include Kalikan, carved into titanic columns of stone supporting a vast cavern; Matikla, the first city and home to the oldest temple; Rokos, the deep place where Dark Elves trade with the things that live in the deeper darkness; and Renekon, which sits on an island in the Great Waterfall that pours into the bottomless Abyss.

SOCIAL ORGANIZATION

Dark Elf society is divided in two classes: those who can bear the constant whispers imposed by Malassa's mark and those who can't. The Dark Elves that can't channel the permanent flow of information are forced to erect a barrier to shield themselves from the rest of the world. Those who successfully process the voices from the Darkness without losing their mind hold great power and play a major political role.

When they settled in Ygg-Chall, the Dark Elves organized themselves into several clans, each led by a child of Tuidhana. What unites them however are not blood relationships, but a common interest for a specific message found in the whispers. Members of the Nightshard clan are passionate about emotions like sadness or happiness. The Shadowbrand clan listens for secrets of the soul. The Soulscar clan is fascinated by pain, suffering and madness.

PHYSCIAL DESCRIPTION

Dark Elves are similar to their forest cousins, but with a paler skin. Hair and eye colour vary widely, but many dye their hair purple, as homage to Tuidhana (who had amethyst-coloured eyes).

Dark Elves usually dress in black. Their armour is often made of black leather, lizard hides, or scale-mail. They don't use Starsilver like the Wood Elves, but rather Shadowsteel, the enchanted metal that is found in the deepest bowels of Ashan.

RACIAL ABILITIES

Like their forest cousins, Dark Elves have heightened senses and are very agile. They have developed night vision which allows them to see in the dark, but makes them very sensitive to sunlight. The knowledge they amass while listening to the Darkness confers them a deep understanding of their enemies, which they use to anticipate and manipulate their actions. Combined with their acute sense and reflexes, it functions as a preternatural awareness that gives them a real edge over their adversaries.

DIPLOMACY

EXTERNAL RELATIONS WITH OTHER FACTIONS

Historical allies: none

Historical enemies: Fortress (the Dwarves), Sylvan (the Wood Elves), Haven (the Knights – Dark Elves are branded as enemies by the Church of Light because they worship Malassa, the Dragon of Darkness)

ACADEMY

When they seek forbidden knowledge, they come to us. Each thinks he is the only one. We know better, and we bind each one who comes to us to our service.

FORTRESS

Let them think they have defeated us. Sooner or later their vigilance will grow lax, and then we will take our revenge.

NECROPOLIS

Death is just one aspect of Darkness. They have found the road, and turned away from it.

SYLVAN

We will cover their sky in darkness and watch as their forests wither. Some things cannot be forgotten, or forgiven.

HAVEN

Proud and foolish. Their Light only illuminates half of existence. Give them enough time and they will destroy themselves.

INFERNO

Darkness smothers fire. This is something they have not yet learned.

STRONGHOLD

They reject the power of the dragons because they have not felt it. Once we show them the majesty of darkness, they will walk the true path.

SANCTUARY

The shadows are everywhere; both above and below the water. Malassa knows all that they know, and more; let them steep in their waters while their wisdom is laid bare.

INTERNAL DISSENSIONS

Dark Elves have a natural taste for the mastery of information, and as a result it is very hard for them to fight each other: each belligerent would anticipate the others' actions and since everything can be known from the whispers, inner struggles would be a terrible waste of time and energy.

However some Dark Elf clans did not remain true to Malassa. In 702 YSD, as the War Under the Mountain turned against the Dark Elves, Raelag, Tuidhana's elder son, signed a pact with exiled Demonists from the Seven Cities. His clan, the Soulscar, turned to secret Demon worship. They became the Demons' elite agents on Ashan, working as messengers and spies in the name of Chaos, keeping an eye on all that happens on the surface.

CULTURE

CORE PHILOSOPHY

"We rule the shadows, and someday the shadows will rule everything".

RELIGION

The Dark Elves worship Malassa, the Dragon of Darkness, Keeper of Secrets.

MAGIC

Dark Elves favour Dark Magic, the "alien" magic of the mysterious, unfathomable shadows. Coils of darkness reach out to smite their enemies, torches extinguish themselves, blindness descends on enemy eyes. Other spells specialize in deception and stealth, and the most powerful summon the spirit of the void itself, to feed on the willpower of their enemies.

ARCHITECTURE

Dark Elf buildings are generally renovations or extensions of ancient Faceless ruins, built in stone and crystal. They are also a conscious rejection of the fluid organic style that the wood Elves prefer. The structures are angular, all right angles and sharp lines, a conscious scar on the landscape of the caves. Dark Elf cities are heavily decorated with statues, frescoes, bas-relief, glyphs, etc... Windows are high and narrow, the better to filter the incoming light or prevent assassins from climbing in.

The Dark Elf artists find their inspiration in drug-induced visions and trances. They are also heavily influenced by their Faceless mentors. The result is a "surrealistic" approach, with strange, twisted creatures and shapes. The largest effigies are that of Malassa and of the martyr-queen Tuidhana.

The temple of Malassa is generally the central building, soaring as high as the cavern ceiling will allow.

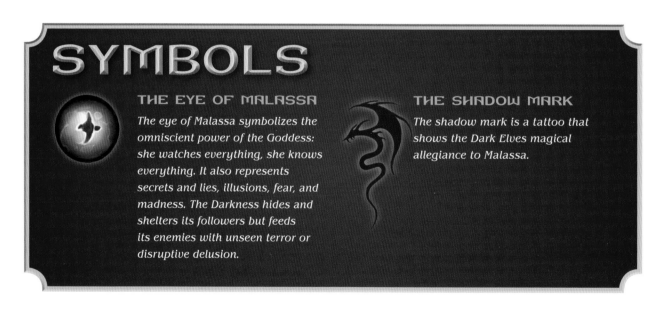

SYMBOLS

THE EYE OF MALASSA

The eye of Malassa symbolizes the omniscient power of the Goddess: she watches everything, she knows everything. It also represents secrets and lies, illusions, fear, and madness. The Darkness hides and shelters its followers but feeds its enemies with unseen terror or disruptive delusion.

THE SHADOW MARK

The shadow mark is a tattoo that shows the Dark Elves magical allegiance to Malassa.

WARFARE

ON THE BATTLEFIELD

Dark Elves are a pragmatic people, and bribery and assassination are often cheaper than raising an army. Their generals believe that a war is better won with persuasive words, devious stratagems, and poisoned daggers than with an army in the field, and as such they have no hesitation about sending out spies, saboteurs and assassins as instruments of their policy.

Dark Elves can use other tactics as well. The main body of their infantry consists of dispensable slaves (usually Beastmen) or beasts from the darkness. Elite troops are fast-moving skirmishers, armoured in light scale mail and armed with curved sword and throwing daggers.

Support comes from crossbow units and Shadow Sorcerers, who master various mind-control and life-draining spells. If forced to fight in the open, Dark Elves prefer to strike under cover of darkness. If forced to fight in daylight, they can stand their ground, but they're more inclined to retreat and wait for nightfall.

The most famous weapons of the Dark Elves are their crossbows, cut from the roots of a Treant, their trigger and mechanism forged from Shadowsteel. They shoot further, send quarrels truer, and inflict more grievous wounds than any regular bow or crossbow.

ICONIC DUNGEON HERO

THE SHADOW SORCERER

Servants of Malassa, the Shadow Sorcerers are seekers of forbidden lore and masters of Dark Magic. They totally accept the murmurs of the Darkness and are capable of finding the information that they want. Those who rise to the highest ranks undergo a secret ritual that lets them commune directly with Malassa, making them capable of dreamwalking. When the ritual is complete, their eyes become black and pupiless, and they never blink again.

ICONIC DUNGEON ALLIES

SHADOW LURKER

The Shadow Lurker is a minor Spirit of Darkness in the shape of a floating orb of shadows with a single central purple and glowing eye and several eyestalks framing its body like tentacles, each ending in a smaller eye. It is said these beings are born in Malassa's dark wings, before detaching themselves to wander in the subterranean realms. Like the goddess, they can hear the murmurs of the shadows. Some Dark Elves use them to harness even more information.

MANTICORE

The Manticore is a Magical Beast created by the magic emanating from an underground Dragon vein (a concentration of dragonblood crystals that forms a Nexus of magical energies). In the Manticore's case, the Nexus is attuned to the Elemental Dragon of Darkness. The Manticore is notorious for its venomous stinger. The Dark Elves extract this poison to impregnate their weapons.

MINOTAUR

Minotaurs are fusions of man and bull who were created in the laboratories of the Seven Cities, alongside other Beastmen such as Harpies and Centaurs. Originally created as shock infantry to fight alongside the Centaur cavalry. The Crimson Wizards of Karthal, in a diplomatic gesture that surprised many and angered their neighbours (the Silver Cities, the Holy Falcon Empire, and the Elves of Irollan), made a gift of one thousand loyal Minotaurs to the Elves of Tuidhana. The Dark Elves, who appreciated their strength and loyalty, gave them freedom instead of using them as slaves.

SANCTUARY BOOK
THE LOTUS EMPIRE

SUMMARY DESCRIPTION

IN A NUTSHELL

The Nagas are reptilian humanoids living in a mystical and military feudal culture. They are equally at home on land and in the sea, though they move faster in the water. Viewing their time upon Ashan as fleeting and illusory, they strive for perfection in their behaviour and skills. The ideals of purity, simplicity, and harmony are reflected in their magic, their warfare, and their life philosophy.

Aka: The Nagas, the Dragonkin, the Snake people
Associated Colours: Jade green, turquoise and silver
Country / Kingdom: Hashima
Capital City: Nariya, the Eight-petal Lotus

HISTORY

Created as the chosen people of Shalassa, Dragon Goddess of Water, the Nagas are one of the Elder Races of Ashan. Their written and oral histories go back to the time of the Shantiri Empire, which they remember well. The Nagas were appreciated for their harmony, art, and diligence. The Elder Wars, however, took a terrible toll on them. They felt they would be safe in their undersea palaces of shell and coral, but they were more vulnerable than they realized to the wars of Light and Darkness. Centuries had been needed to erect their colossal cities, and only a few years of war to destroy them. By the time the Elder Wars ended, therefore, the Nagas had retreated

into the ice floes and the ocean depths, eschewing all relations with the untrustworthy servant races of the other Dragon Gods. They heard echoes of the studies of Sar-Elam, of course, and quickly read the signs that resulted from his actions. Many warriors and priests left the ruined cities of the deep to seek and study the changes in the world. Discoveries of great wonders of Shalassa above the sea drew more and more followers. The period that saw the first Demon invasion in the rest of the world is therefore known as The Diaspora to the Nagas.

Little by little, the Nagas transformed themselves. Many of their far-flung temples and great city-rafts were founded at this time. But in spite of their increasing presence across the surface of Ashan, the Nagas remained apart, meditating in isolation and perfecting their martial arts. The Naga isolationism became almost a second religion, and the early Eclipses and Demon wars were only heard as echoes and rumours. However, the arrival of the Orcs, led by Kunyak, at the shores of their kingdom shook them awake.

Forced by the light of day to see the truth that the world they had isolated themselves from no longer existed, Nagas renewed contacts with other nations, learning that some would come in peace, some to trade, some to exploit... and some to conquer.

HASHIMA

PAO
ISLANDS

GEOGRAPHIC LOCATION

You will find the Nagas anywhere that you find water, as in all of its forms, it is holy to them. Naga temples are built near waterfalls, lake beds, river rapids, reefs, and in the depths of the ocean. The realms of Shalassa also extend up into the glaciers and through the ice caps, and many of her Naga disciples feel quite at home in these environments.

Some Nagas even live on rafts, floating island temples lashed together from seaweed and driftwood, that are forever circumnavigating Ashan. It is therefore difficult to point to a map and say, "Nagas are here", though one could certainly point to the Sahaar desert and say: "Here, the Nagas are not." And even then, in an oasis...

THE ETERNAL EMPRESS

The Nagas are led by the Eternal Empress. She has ruled as theocrat and benevolent dictator since the mythic Age. She is both the military and spiritual head of Naga society. She appears ageless, but has never been defeated in a duel - with arms, poetry, song, or ceremony. The leaders of the Naga people must be the epitome of perfection in all of their pursuits.

KUNYAK'S ENCOUNTER

When Kunyak and the Orcs descended to take over the Pao Islands, they ran across a small Naga temple at the foot of a great waterfall. Surrounded by his personal bodyguards, Kunyak told the lone Naga warrior on guard to leave or die. The Naga simply pulled his four swords and waited. Kunyak, impressed by his fearless courage, offered to spare his life. The Naga, however, refused.

"How could I worship Shalassa, if I feared death?" he said. "If it is my time to return to the waters, I will do so gladly."

Kunyak would not be stopped by a single soldier, and the Naga was killed. But the temple remains untouched, and many Orcs seek a blessing there before going to battle.

SOCIAL ORGANIZATION

The Naga nation is based on a master-apprentice relationship. All Nagas swear allegiance and promise obedience to their chosen master. Duty and loyalty are expected. When a Naga feels that he has surpassed his master, he must defeat him in a formal duel. If successful, he becomes a master himself, or seeks further training from a superior master. These duels are not necessarily fought with weapons. They could be contests of poetry, ritual meditation, or even cooking.

The highest master in Naga society is the Eternal Empress, who is considered as the living incarnation of Shalassa.

PHYSICAL DESCRIPTION

Nagas have humanoid heads and torsos, but a snake's lower body and tail. It is not uncommon for them to be born with four arms. Their skin is scaly. Like snakes, they have slanted eyes with vertical elliptical pupils. Their tongue, however, is normal, not forked. Female Nagas have "snake-hair". Most of the time, the snakes are asleep, and arranged in an elaborate topknot. But a strong and unexpected emotion or danger can wake them up.

Nagas come in three varieties:

- The **Coral Nagas** are small, like human children, but when they stand on their tail, they can rise up to 5 and a half or 6 feet. Their scales are bright and multi-coloured, and their faces are almost human. They dwell in lagoons and on seashores.

- The **Lake Nagas** are average in size (measuring around 6 feet tall when coiled, and 10 feet long to the tip of their tail). Their scales are of a pale blue-green colour, with brighter streaks, and their faces are more "ophidian" than those of the Coral Nagas. They are found in lakes, large rivers, and marshes.
- The **Deep Nagas** are very big (counting the tail, they can measure from 12 to 15 feet in length). Their scales are dark, and their faces are more reptilian than human. They reside in underwater cities at the bottom of the ocean.

RACIAL ABILITIES

Nagas are amphibian; at home in water or on land. They also have a heightened sense of smell and taste, and they can detect body heat from afar. Their snake tail makes them somewhat slow on even ground, but very nimble when climbing rocks or trees, and extremely fast when swimming in deep water.

NAGA AND TEA

Though various forms of kelp and algae had always been part of the Naga diet, they did not begin creating beverages with them until they began to live more regularly on the surface of Ashan. Needless to say, it is difficult to both dry tea leaves and boil water undersea.

The habit was first picked up from scattered human wanderers living along the shores of the Jade Sea; certain plants when dried and macerated created beverages that were uniquely pleasing to the Nagas' taste buds. The Nagas' study of plants and cultivation of leaves went through a period of explosive growth during the diaspora; many of the great island rafts that were formed traded in tea plants from various parts of Ashan. The first trials that blended dried kelps with dry-land shrubs were made at this point.

Over the last few centuries tea has become an integral part of Naga culture, and its artisans have even crafted special elongated pots which, when filled partially with air and inverted, allow tea to be drunk underwater. A typical temple or inn may offer one or more of the following common traditional Naga teas in addition to local specialties :

Urago - a green tea, named for the hills on the coast northeast of Hashima where the leaves are picked

Heijin - a very dark and smoky tea, rumoured to have excellent restorative qualities

Ohlae - one of the very first blended teas, made from a local kelp from Hashima and leaves from the Austral Islands

Higan - a very particular blended tea, whose leaves are simultaneously sun- and air-dried in the polar regions during winter

Akari - a strong reddish tea, whose leaves are fermented three times before being dried

DIPLOMACY

EXTERNAL RELATIONS WITH OTHER FACTIONS

Historical allies: While the Nagas have had limited contact with other nations of Ashan (primarily through trades or formal embassies), they are most akin to Sylvan (the Harmony-minded Elves of the forests) and Stronghold (the Orcs, whom they respect for their brute courage and honesty, and with whom they share a total indifference to death).

Historical enemies: Inferno (the Demons have an innate distaste for the Nagas' quiet and harmonious nature); Necropolis (Death is simply to be accepted, not worshipped as an ideal state), Fortress (the Nagas find the Dwarves loud, rude, and smelly; in addition they feel little affection for the Dragon of Fire).

ACADEMY

They seek purity and perfection, but they do so in laboratories and books. They do not see that mind, body, and nature must be as one.

INFERNO

They do not understand duty, or seek purity, or appreciate wisdom. The endless waves of Shalassa shall drown them one day.

NECROPOLIS

Death is neither to be adored nor bent to one's will, one must merely accept its inevitability. The obsession of the Necromancers is misguided and foolish.

HAVEN

Little more than grown-up Dwarves, the Knights at least understand manners and politeness. A pity that their fanaticism limits their minds.

FORTRESS

The Dwarves are loud and arrogant; their humour is coarse and their culture is simple. They stink of fumes and fire. Keep them away.

SYLVAN

Their reverence for the earth is worthy of respect; woe that they understand so little of the sea.

DUNGEON

The seas contain both shadow and light; the much-adored secrets of the Dark Elves are but half-truths based on ignorance, not wisdom.

STRONGHOLD

They are fierce and honourable – in their own brutal ways. Like us, they do not fear death. If we could teach them how to cool their anger and focus their spirit, they could join us on the path of perfect balance.

A TEACUP OF WISDOM

Imperial Ambassador: *Your culture is fascinating to us. We would like to learn more.*

Naga diplomat: *First, we shall have some tea.*

(The Naga pours tea, and continues pouring after the ambassadors cup is full).

Imperial Ambassador: *What are you doing!?*

Naga diplomat: *Like the teacup, your mind is already full of what you think you know. You must empty your mind. Then we may speak of the ways of Shalassa.*

CULTURE

CORE PHILOSOPHY

"Blend the pure waters of heaven and the bitter waters of the ocean with your own. Unite yourself to the endless sea. Empty yourself and let the Divine function".

RELIGION

The Nagas worship Shalassa, the Dragon of Water, in all its aspects (oceans, lakes, brooks, springs, rain, mist, snow, ice, blood and tears...).

MAGIC

Nagas are masters of the "quiet" magic sphere of Water, that renders the body and the mind as malleable as a liquid. They place much store in wisdom and in study. For this reason, their magic tends to work over time and build gradually to a smashing crescendo. Attack spells may echo the effects of tidal waves or hurricanes; blessings permit the troops to attack in unstoppable waves; curses leave the enemy slowed and off balanced.

NAGA RIDDLE

Naga pilgrim: *Tell me, master. Is the sea moving the wave, or does the wave move the sea?*

Kirin: *Neither one, tadpole. It is your mind that moves.*

ARCHITECTURE

Undersea or on the coasts, Naga structures are built from natural materials. While the Nagas are perfectly comfortable on the land, it is clear that their true home is the sea. Though they do not quite have the skill that the Elves show with the trees, the coral reefs and mother-of-pearl columns of Naga undersea houses are grown as much as they are constructed. The shapes echo the forms and features of marine life and geology.

Their simple land structures also show similar decorations, and are built with the materials they know best – rocks from river or sea beds, alluvial clays, reeds, and driftwoods. If land structures last only a few years it is of no consequence to them. The Nagas believe that as the sea moves, so everything moves; change is permanent and unceasing and inevitable.

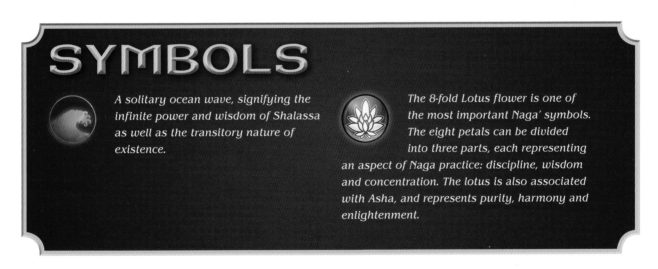

SYMBOLS

A solitary ocean wave, signifying the infinite power and wisdom of Shalassa as well as the transitory nature of existence.

The 8-fold Lotus flower is one of the most important Naga' symbols. The eight petals can be divided into three parts, each representing an aspect of Naga practice: discipline, wisdom and concentration. The lotus is also associated with Asha, and represents purity, harmony and enlightenment.

WARFARE

ON THE BATTLEFIELD

Strike where your enemy is the strongest, fearing no challenge for there is no honourable fight you cannot win and no honourable death Shalassa might blame you for. Once your enemy's blade is broken, all you'll need is a mercy strike to end the quarrel.

The Naga warfare is all about control and an iron arm. Control to ensure the enemy cannot reach one's most vital assets or at least not too early. An iron arm to ensure that, where contact will take place, the Nagas will be the strongest. As amphibians, the Nagas are most at ease fighting on wet or watery ground; their natural forms are so well adapted to this that any enemy is at a great disadvantage. They will always try to bring the fight on this kind of terrain.

As they are largely indifferent to death, believing that they will be reborn to serve Shalassa in a higher form, the Nagas seldom feel the need to run from battle or save themselves. As a result, it is more likely that a Naga army will be decimated than surrender. This fearless character, tempered by wisdom and an implacable serenity, is a potent weapon. In times of trouble, there will always be a champion to move calmly towards the enemy and draw any danger to himself, giving his companions time to prepare themselves and gain tactical advantage.

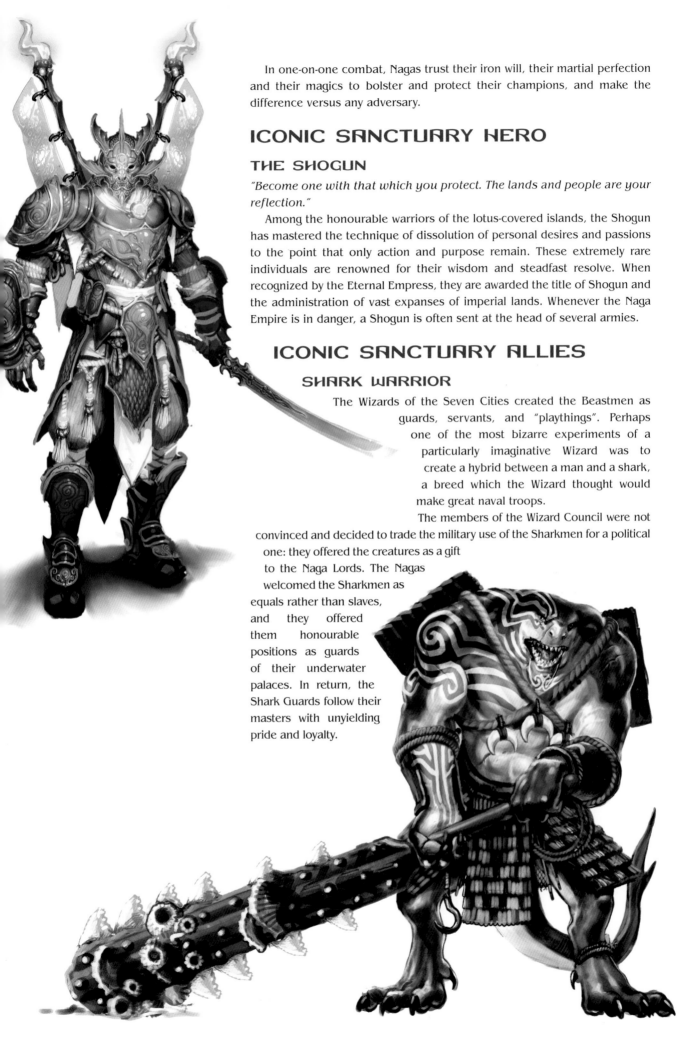

In one-on-one combat, Nagas trust their iron will, their martial perfection and their magics to bolster and protect their champions, and make the difference versus any adversary.

ICONIC SANCTUARY HERO

THE SHOGUN

"Become one with that which you protect. The lands and people are your reflection."

Among the honourable warriors of the lotus-covered islands, the Shogun has mastered the technique of dissolution of personal desires and passions to the point that only action and purpose remain. These extremely rare individuals are renowned for their wisdom and steadfast resolve. When recognized by the Eternal Empress, they are awarded the title of Shogun and the administration of vast expanses of imperial lands. Whenever the Naga Empire is in danger, a Shogun is often sent at the head of several armies.

ICONIC SANCTUARY ALLIES

SHARK WARRIOR

The Wizards of the Seven Cities created the Beastmen as guards, servants, and "playthings". Perhaps one of the most bizarre experiments of a particularly imaginative Wizard was to create a hybrid between a man and a shark, a breed which the Wizard thought would make great naval troops.

The members of the Wizard Council were not convinced and decided to trade the military use of the Sharkmen for a political one: they offered the creatures as a gift to the Naga Lords. The Nagas welcomed the Sharkmen as equals rather than slaves, and they offered them honourable positions as guards of their underwater palaces. In return, the Shark Guards follow their masters with unyielding pride and loyalty.

KAPPA

Often jokingly described as the offspring of a toad and a turtle, Kappas are in truth minor Water Spirits linked to the rivers and lakes, bound to a material shape by their alliance with the Naga priesthood. Travellers from other lands often make fun of the Kappa's appearance and demeanour, but the Nagas know better and never underestimate the martial talents of these strange creatures.

KIRIN

A powerful Water Spirit linked to the celestial waters in all their aspects (rain, hail, clouds, fog, mist...), the Kirin is known in the Naga culture as the bringer of wisdom and chooser of lords. It is said that a warlord who brings a Kirin to battle is blessed by Shalassa and the whole army benefits from the spirit's heavenly aura. It is also said that one who rides the Kirin may travel faster than the wind, but at the cost of his own life.